Alpha for the Pack

The Stars of the Pack - Book II
N.J. LYSK

I0679670

Palm Hearts
PalmHeartsBooks@gmail.com
ISBN: 978-1-916630-04-8

The Stars of the Pack series (Chronologically)

0.1) Midnight Encounters*
1) Omega for the Pack
1.1) Simpler than Most*
2) Alpha for the Pack
3) Protectors of the Pack
4) Beloved of the Pack
4.1) Shock Therapy*
5) Betas Aside
5.1) Around the Hearth*
\= Interludes/extras that don't need to be read to follow.

Companion series:
Runt of the Litter
Paper Kisses

Also available in German, French, Italian, Dutch, Spanish, Portuguese and bilingual learner editions

Alpha for the Pack

Prologue

E ven with six of them, five newborns were a handful. But Ray, Josh and Gabriel had experience with kids and Alec had been through a paediatric internship as part of his degree. And Sergi and Iesu were, in one word, devoted. Once, at the very beginning, Ray had started to explain about diaper rash—it went away quickly in werewolves, but babies would still make a fuss about it—and Sergi had stopped him and asked for a minute to go get pen and paper.

Ray waited, but mostly he tried not to argue when they were all so tired already. Ray had finished secondary school a year ago, and dropped off college two weeks after starting when he'd presented. And Sergi thought he should take *notes* when he spoke. Given, it was about the babies and Ray had four younger siblings he had helped raise but... He had finished his explanation before cornering his mate. "There's books about this kind of thing, you know?"

Instead of excited, Sergi had looked guilty. "Fuck, of course there are, I should have—"

"No!" Ray took hold of his arm to keep him from running off, probably to drive to the nearest bookshop. "That's not what I meant. I just..." He gestured at the notebook Sergi still held. "If you are writing down *my* advice..."

Sergi's dark eyes softened, it made Ray want to look away. He was almost unrecognizable from the boy who'd teased Ray so cruelly less than a year ago.

"Hey," he said, smile soft like a caress, but he didn't touch Ray back. Not casually like Gabriel did, like they were the kind of lovers who'd asked each other for permission too many times already. Ray liked it, that he didn't assume he had a right. But he didn't know how to tell him he wanted to be touched sometimes, that he wanted the tenderness he saw on Sergi's face on his skin. "You give very good advice. Could write a book all of your own."

Ray snorted, smiling despite himself. "Fuck off," he told Sergi, so softly the words sounded a little absurd, and Sergi laughed too.

He went to Alec himself when the third full moon passed with just some running. So unlike the first full moon after the pups had been born—when the alphas had barely been able to keep their hands off him—and even the passionate sex of the second, that Ray couldn't help but worry. He had to worry because the other choice was to hope. And he couldn't afford to hope to spend many full moons with his pups and his mates, running around, taking turns keeping them corralled and away from danger. Chasing but just in play, catching some rabbits, and teaching the pups where the tender spots were.

It had felt... It had been nice, but Ray knew it couldn't last.

"It's been three months." He flopped down on Alec's bed. There was no point beating around the bush. He had no time for it anyway; he was still breastfeeding twice a day, even though they were already starting the babies on solid food. Thank god for werewolf metabolism; Ray couldn't imagine what it'd have been like to keep them on a liquid diet for half a year or more. Of course, if he wasn't a werewolf... Still, he was grateful for small mercies.

Alec looked up from his computer. He had told Ray to come in, but he hadn't looked at him until now. "Yes," he agreed a little tentatively. He looked ethereal with the late afternoon sun illuminating his light copper hair from behind. His soft features and big eyes made him look younger than he was, younger than Ray felt—despite being five years Alec's junior. Alec had put off mating for as long as he'd been able to, just like Gabriel, because he wasn't attracted to women.

"So will it happen on the next full moon? Last week was great, but you said..." Ray tugged at the blankets on Alec's bed, fixing very little since he was still on top of them.

"I don't really know, Ray," Alec said. "I figured there might be some signs right before, but right now... Well, last week the pups were there. I haven't talked to the others, but for me... I don't think I could, not anywhere near them, even if they don't understand."

Ray sighed. "Thank the Goddess for that, at least. But wouldn't that mean that if they run with us...?"

"I—No," Alec said, sounding so pained all Ray could do was look away. "Mated wolves run with the pack, but they find a secluded space for... If you were in heat, we would have to. And they're starting on solid food, even if they still like milk."

Ray knew well what that meant: what little protection his own body offered him while his pups were young enough to need his full attention was wearing out. He shifted in place, hunching over his still swollen tits. It'd become so normal for him that he managed to forget about it most of the time, but talking about it always made him self-conscious.

"Is there anything I can do?" he asked. Sometimes he thought all he could do was take it, whatever happened. He had worked so hard to be okay with this, with the alphas and the babies and most of all himself, and now...

"Yeah!" Alec sounded desperate to offer some good news. He stood from his desk as if he meant to approach, then simply leaned back against it. Ray saw his hands were digging into the wooden surface, he wanted to tell him it wasn't necessary. But it was, if Alec touched him then... Alec's voice was even. "I mean; I think it'll work like any heat. If we do it before and get it out of our systems when you're not... I think that would help bring things down a notch."

Ray sighed, disappointed. Alec had been right in the past: it did help to have sex with his alphas more frequently right before heat. It helped the *alphas*, at least. It wouldn't help Ray when his wolf went into heat and dragged him along for the ride. It had been a year and he could still remember it, not just the general rush of the full moon but an actual heat.

"But those heats, I was already..." He trailed off. He never said the word anymore, not even when speaking about other people. It was always 'so and so are having a baby', 'expecting' at the most. It was the same thing, of course, but the 'p' word set him on edge. It brought back the feeling of it for Ray: the fullness and discomfort, the alphas' desperate need to claim him again and again.

"Yes," Alec agreed. "But I told you, the fact that you were pregnant made it worse. The wolves... It's like they don't believe it until they can feel it, and during the full moon..."

Ray knew what he meant. He hadn't gone into heat after the first time. At least not the kind of heat he had experienced right after presenting omega, when he had been so gone on hormones he had happily spread his legs for five alphas. But even after he'd conceived, the alphas had needed him just as badly.

The full moon brought every one of the wolf's needs to the forefront: sex and hunting became everything. With five alphas bent on having him, Ray's body had burned with *their* desire. That was how omegas functioned: adapting to their alphas' needs and desires down to their very biology.

Alec kept talking, "But for an alpha, well, fucking and knotting are different types of sex."

Ray straightened on the bed and gave himself a moment before asking, "You mean you didn't have to...?" He couldn't say it. He wasn't even sure he wanted to know. He had thought they didn't have a choice about knotting him during the full-moon, if they had and they still had done it to him... He didn't want to be angry with them, or worse. He needed them too much for that. He had come to—

"No!" Alec raised both hands and rushed to explain, "We had to! During a bonding heat? We had no bloody choice, even if it wasn't required for bonding itself. But maybe, I don't know, we might be able to stop ourselves from knotting during heat. When it comes back, I mean. The wolves know you are their mate now. It's difficult because..." He swallowed, looking uncomfortable and flushed. "But alphas have done it. I asked around, and it's possible. And we'll try. We all want you to be happy, Ray. But it'd help a lot if we had sex before things get crazy. I mean, we don't have to, I'm not—"

"Like, the day before?" Ray interrupted before Alec could dig himself any deeper into a hole. He wasn't telling Ray to do it, or at least he didn't want to be, but he was presenting all the data that made having sex with him the only reasonable option Ray had. Ray could have asked somebody else about it, an omega, even. But he could hear Alec's heartbeat, the accelerated rate revealed his nerves, but it hadn't stuttered once while he spoke. He wasn't lying.

"I... I don't really know," Alec said, shrugging. He turned back to the computer and disconnected his USB drive for no reason Ray could see. He plugged it back in. "I'm—"

"Alec, stop treating me like I'm fragile," he demanded. He didn't want to get angry at Alec—it wasn't like he had any more control over the situation than Ray did—but all this talking around it really didn't help. Not because he wasn't fragile, he felt about to shatter into a million pieces, but because he had finally realised that the truth couldn't be worse than what he had overheard and assumed—and at least it had the advantage of actually predicting reality. "*Tell me.*"

"A week," Alec blurted out, turning his way but keeping his gaze averted. "A week might be enough."

Ray exhaled, bending forward to put his hands on his knees. Alec didn't say anything, and he knew he had understood correctly: to take the edge off enough so they didn't feel the need to breed him during heat, he was going to have to put up with getting fucked by the five of them each night for a week. And that *might* do it, it also might not be enough.

And he had to try. Not just for himself, really, he didn't think they were ready to deal with even more chaos than five babies that could both crawl and run brought. Two days earlier, Maria had figured out she could shift without Ray doing it, and it wouldn't be long before her siblings followed her example.

He had a couple of days anyway. He could ease himself into it.

It seemed like a good plan, even if it meant an end to the restful life he had gotten used to lately.

So, of course, it went to hell in a hand basket as soon as they decided to put it into practice. Two days later, Ray was lying in bed with a book of reproductions Iesu had unearthed from somewhere when Josh came in to tell him they needed to talk to him.

Ray hadn't expected good news; he hadn't had many of those since presenting. Maybe excepting the fact that even if his alphas fucked him through heat, he probably wouldn't get pregnant as long as the babies were feeding off him. Maybe not even that, the way his chest also hurt from werewolf babies' early teething.

He put the book down and waited for the all the alphas to fill in, feeling dread pooling in his stomach as the room got smaller with their presence. They all preferred if one of them was with the pups at all times, even if it was perfectly safe to leave them in another room for a few minutes, so the news must be important enough to warrant an exception.

"We've had a request to join the pack," Gabriel said formally. He had been right, from Gabriel that kind of stuffiness couldn't be good news. "And we have got to put it to you, as first omega."

"We wouldn't ask, Ray, but you know we need more pack members and nobody wants to join a new pack," Josh sounded like the words pained him to say as much as it pained Ray to hear them. And Ray wasn't even sure he was understood what he was being asked.

"What are you asking exactly?"

"There's six of them," Gabriel explained, maybe as a kindness to Josh, maybe because he wanted to get it over with as soon as possible for all their sakes'. "They want to join us, but they want you to take their leader."

"As a mate?"

"No!" Sergi sounded furious. "You are *our* mate."

Ray sighed, put upon by their vagueness. "What are you talking about then?"

"A breeding," Alec explained, failing miserably to sound professional as he added, "Just the once."

"You want me to let..." Ray trailed off, feeling oddly... hurt. He had thought they liked him, at least. Respected him as their mate, at the very minimum. And they were asking him to spread for a stranger, not just that, to...

"We *don't*," Josh said fiercely. "But you're the omega, it's your decision who joins the pack. And you need to know what they are asking, so you can decide if you want to talk to them."

Ray stared, torn between laughing and crying. *His decision?*

Chapter 1

B ut in truth, it was his decision. Ray couldn't choose what his body did, and he couldn't settle disputes for territory, but as first omega of his pack, he could tell them how far the territory extended, where every member of the pack was, and whether the pack needed more members.

He wondered how omegas normally knew something like that, whether they sat with their mate and discussed it... For Ray, it was simple maths; he might avoid a pregnancy this full moon and the next, but he wouldn't avoid it for much longer and then, less than a year in the future, he'd have a pack with ten kids under five. In two years it might be fifteen. And six adults.

It just wouldn't work. They needed other omegas and betas too, younger or older, who were unencumbered by children of their own. But no beta would just join a new pack, and no omega *could* join a new pack that couldn't provide an alpha for them. And it was only natural that alphas would want children of their own.

The visiting alphas were a group of twenty-somethings who'd left their own packs cities away to explore the land and find some adventure. It wasn't surprising Ray's small pack had attracted their attention. Ray knew he might owe their safety to his uncle's large pack right across the lake. If it hadn't been for them, they'd have looked like a better target than ally...

But he couldn't afford to be thinking like that, not just before meeting their leader.

The man was waiting in the main room of the house. The room was large enough for a table where they could all eat together—although they'd probably need a separate kids' table soon enough—and some sofas and a TV on the other end. They hadn't wanted to waste space putting a wall in between so it was closer in size to a small school auditorium than a living room. And with just the strange alpha and Ray there, it felt echoingly empty.

The man had been patiently watching the front door when Ray walked in. He had curly, dark blonde hair and sharp features, not unattractive, Ray supposed, but nothing special. Then he stood up and revealed a set of shoulders Ray could have worked at a gym for half his life without achieving.

He offered Ray his hand, tense but not nervous, polite but not condescending. Ray shook it. Many alphas wouldn't have dared touch a claimed omega, even if that omega had the deciding vote on whether they were allowed into a pack. His grip was firm and brief, and even though he was affected by touching Ray, he didn't let it show in his expression. "Raymond, right? I'm Nicholas."

Ray nodded. "Take a seat," he ordered. Nicholas might have been an alpha, but he was in Ray's territory, every inch of it like a part of his body, and Ray was owed his respect for the honour.

The alpha sat and tilted his head to look up at Ray without any apparent discomfort at leaving his neck exposed. Not that he was really at risk, Ray knew he wasn't capable of killing him—probably wouldn't have been even before the draining experience of a pregnancy, childbirth, and hourly feedings. "Talk to me about your... pack."

"Never called ourselves that," Nicholas said calmly, not rising to the bait. "No pack without an omega."

Any posturing aside, having to look up at Ray, who was no giant but stood over six foot tall, couldn't have been comfortable. But Nicholas kept his posture relaxed and his eyes on his face. "And now you want one? Why did you leave your birth pack?"

"It wasn't that long ago, really. I was bored with the whole thing. Have you ever been to Manchester?" Ray shook his head. He'd been to London once with his school. And he'd wanted to visit other big cities, maybe even to live there for a while. He'd figured he had time; he'd finish school and then... But it turned out he didn't. He'd run out of time to see the world the moment he'd become an omega, the moment he'd bonded not just with his alphas, but with the land as well.

Nicholas shrugged. "Well, it's a little bit too industrialized for werewolves, but we make do and all. Except it's getting more and more crowded, and the only way to live there is to stay human all the time—"

"And that's a problem?" Ray asked. It came out too sharp, but he'd heard of packs who'd gone feral and moved to a remote location to live off the land. It did not end well. They couldn't be just wolves, just like they couldn't be just humans.

Nicholas looked up again. "Well, yeah. Obviously, I wouldn't want to be a wolf full-time, either. But in the city, finding the time to shift is like finding the time to go hiking, or on a holiday. I don't think it should be like that. I like what you guys got here." Ray was still watching him, thinking through it, when Nicholas spoke again, "Come on, don't tell me you don't like shifting whenever you like; why else do you live in the middle of nowhere?"

"I was born here," Ray replied neutrally.

Nicholas hummed, conceding the point. "The big pack across the lake, right?"

Ray nodded, suddenly at a loss about what to ask. Nicholas saw it right away. "Do you want to sit down so I can tell you about the guys?"

Ray hesitated, but there was a difference between being in control and being childish. He wasn't an alpha, after all; there was no need for posturing. He sat. Nicholas smiled at him, soft and pleased like Ray had given him something instead of merely sitting down and agreeing to listen. In a way, it was true, Ray had given him this chance, even if they both knew Ray needed it just as much as he did.

"You—" Nicholas started to say, then closed his mouth and looked away. "I'm from a big family. Two dads," he added by way of explanation. "Or four, I guess, but the point is that I'm good with kids." He glanced at the toys scattered in a corner of the room. "And I'm not bad with cars either, did a module and I like to play around with them. Might come in handy around these parts."

Ray had assumed he was in his late twenties, but now he was starting to doubt it. He didn't sound it when he talked about himself. The man wasn't short on accomplishments, but he didn't have any practice listing them.

"Are the others from your birth pack?" he asked, hoping to redirect his attention.

Nicholas looked up. "Clyde and Rob are, grew up together. Always got them in trouble," he told Ray with a fond smile. "Rama and—"

"Stop," Ray demanded. It was insane. Six men, six men he *had never even met,* and he was thinking of letting them... He only realised he was breathing heavily when the alpha went to his knees at his feet and clamped a hand around his ankle, hard and impossible to ignore. A grounding presence requiring Ray's attention.

"Raymond, just breathe. I'm just *asking*, you don't have to—"

"I don't have to?!" Ray snapped, not caring if he actually spat on his face. "What the fuck are you talking about? How am I supposed to do this without help?"

"But you have your alphas—"

"It's not enough, no pack can survive with a single omega. Without betas. Who is supposed to go and work for the money we need for supplies if everybody has to stay in to look after the children?"

"Didn't your... I mean, didn't your parents arrange for some betas to come with you when you started the pack?"

"No, it was just us," Ray said, angry still, but unable to stop talking. "Since I was an omega, it was expected I would start a new pack."

"Couldn't you ask them now?"

"Ask?" Ray repeated. "In exchange for what? They're not my pack any longer. I could ask for some money, or a car, or something, but people to work here?"

"Since you were an omega, you said, why... Well, of course you didn't expect it," he said, looking Ray up and down, maybe noticing for the first time he was a big man.

"Yeah, well, gotta get over that quick," Ray said quietly. "I have way bigger problems."

"I'll help you if you want," Nicholas offered. Ray frowned at him.

"Why would you want to? I mean, any pack would take you." He didn't even want to take it back when he realised that he was pretty much saying *he* would, without discussing conditions or anything.

"I stopped for the land," Nicholas said, eyes fixed on him. He was still on the floor, hand around Ray's clothed ankle, but hot through it still. "But I want to stay for you."

Ray stared. He had admitted he needed the alpha, but he hadn't expected a declaration in exchange. "You met me less than half an hour ago, and the only thing you know about me is that I'm desperate."

"And that you're arguing," Nicholas explained. "You need me. Us. But you are arguing anyway. You didn't try to trick me or hide anything from me. I want that."

"Trick you?" Ray repeated. "Who would do that to an alpha they want?"

Nicholas smiled at the implied admission, then shrugged. "Yeah, well, now you know why I wanted to get away," he confessed, looking down. This time he wasn't lost in remembrances or trying to put Ray at ease, this time he didn't want Ray to see his face. His heart-rate was slightly elevated, too, from fear, or pain. Or both.

Ray didn't want to ask. Strangely, he didn't need to know. He'd been hurt too and needed his own time to recover. "But it's just so stupid, almost as stupid as agreeing to… do this with an alpha I just met."

Nicholas laughed dryly at that, sensing Ray's self-deprecating humour through his defeated tone. "Almost as stupid as taking on a pack that's just starting up and trying to build it from the ground up?" he asked in turn, brown eyes shining up at Ray.

Ray nodded. Nicholas straightened, just enough that he was level with Ray's hunched posture. Just enough to meet his eyes, for the first time, from the same height.

"But we are going to do it."

"Yes," Ray said. "We are."

He leaned forward and pushed his mouth against his new alpha's to seal the deal.

"We are hoping it'll be a while before the next litter," Alec explained at dinner. Ray kept his eyes on his food and didn't look at any of the strangers nodding along at the most intimate workings of his body. If he was going to let them mount him—and he would have to do it if he wanted to invite them into the pack—then talking was nothing.

He hadn't mentioned it to Nicholas earlier, but the man sounded thoughtful when he commented, "Those kids of yours are already eating through the fence. Need to get something metallic there before there's more of them."

He next complimented Alec on the meat, like both things were equally innocuous to discuss at dinner. Ray wondered if for him conversations about planning for more children depending on the state of repair of the property were normal, since he was the child of an omega male himself.

Ray hadn't noticed, but Josh admitted later that it was true that the pups had been chewing on the corners of the fence. They were just lucky the little adventurers hadn't figured out they could dig their way out into the great wilderness of the hills. For a while, Ray had looked forward to his kids growing up and becoming more independent; now he was starting to remember his little brother's adventures as a toddler and calling himself an idiot.

It was hard to have strangers crawling all over his land when he could feel them there, and the knowledge that he had agreed to let them *much* closer didn't help. But Ray was dealing, and his alphas were being polite enough—even if they were transparently uncomfortable at being outnumbered and having strange alphas around the babies.

It was just that Ray didn't know what would happen when he told them what he had decided. They'd brought him the proposal because they had to, and on a rational level, they had known he had to seriously consider it. But that didn't mean it wouldn't hurt.

They might not have loved him, but they were his mates and he had promised to be theirs for the rest of his life. Saying yes to Nicholas felt like a betrayal, but if it was necessary to keep them all alive and safe...

He had to tell Josh first, he knew, because for Josh it went beyond instincts. Josh hadn't saved him and left his pack to become Ray's protector because of mating urges. He was as vulnerable to the power of the moon and instinct as Ray himself, but even if Ray could never forgive him for that, he could never forget all the little kindnesses either. He knew he meant something to Josh. As treasonous as it had felt when Josh had offered to be his alpha, he knew Josh had cared for him long before that. He wasn't sure in what way, but Josh loved him. He had known Ray before he had become an omega, and he hadn't abandoned him when he had—and maybe it was... Only it didn't matter, exactly, what it was. Josh had proven his loyalty, and Ray owed it to him to acknowledge it.

It wasn't easy to get him alone, but eventually, he got the last baby fed—Jamie, of course—and made up an excuse about wanting to look up some furniture on the website Josh had been raving about. Josh didn't even go for the computer once the door closed behind them, instead turning to Ray and examining him closely. "What is it?"

Ray swallowed, keeping his gaze averted. His alphas had never made him follow the protocol, but he still found he needed it sometimes. "I'm going to invite them to join the pack."

Josh made a choked noise, then exhaled loudly. Ray looked up to see him clenching his fists, eyes shut tightly as he held his breath for a long moment. His heart was beating so fast it was no wonder he was out of breath when he spoke. "Of course," he said eventually. "I... It's your decision."

But he was too obviously upset for Ray to let it go. "You don't think I should? How else am I supposed to get enough adults in the pack to take care of the children? To provide for all of us?"

"I..." Josh was breathing harshly. "I don't know, Ray. I just..."

"If you don't have any better suggestions—" Ray started to say.

"Oh, god, shut up!" Josh snapped. Ray did, throat closing up even as the surprise paralyzed his brain. Josh immediately backtracked. "Fuck, sorry, I... speak, if you want!" Ray didn't, and Josh gave him a worried look. "It's just a lot to take in. Please don't think I'm... angry or something. I just... didn't expect it."

"Well, you should have, I don't have any other choice," Ray replied bitterly. *He* was angry, he realised. Not with Josh, who had no reason to know better, but with his uncle, who had sent him off into this without enough backup. "Apparently, somebody forgot my complimentary betas when they sent me off to start a new pack."

Josh sat down on the bed, frowning. "Is that a thing? Sending betas? Is that what *Nicholas* said?" He was clearly sceptical and quite as obviously not happy about Nicholas. And except for Alec, Josh had been the friendliest of hosts all along. Ray could just about picture Gabriel's reaction...

"Pretty much," Ray replied. "And I think he's right. There's no way we can do this without betas."

"Then we should get them," Josh replied. "Wouldn't that be better than getting more alphas around?"

"Betas follow alphas, Josh."

"Ray, I can't..." He met Ray's eyes, desperately sincere. "It was bad enough with five. I don't want to see you go through that."

Ray looked away, face burning. His body locked tight—as if he could cut himself off from it and all the pain it'd bring him. "Well, it's my decision."

"But I'm your alpha," Josh said, more plea than statement. "I'm supposed to take care of you, to keep you safe—"

"But you can't," Ray said. "I wish you could, and... I wish there was another way."

"Okay, wait, just..." Ray heard him swallow thickly. "Let me ask. I'll go and ask your uncle. You know he likes me, maybe if I explain that we are not coping so well, he'll let us borrow some betas."

Ray hesitated, but ultimately it was some hope and Josh was asking him for himself as much as for Ray. "Okay, you can ask."

But hope—even one so small as Josh's plan provided—was harder to live with than resignation. Ray felt like a dick asking Nicholas and his friends to clear out for the next full moon. Nicholas had agreed to it in the same conversation in which Ray had promised to tell his alphas that Nicholas would be staying, and now... He might not only not fulfil his promise but instead, tell Nicholas that he had to go.

He didn't really believe his uncle would suddenly remember he had neglected to send any betas with them, apologize for the misunderstanding, and send half a dozen willing babysitters. Josh couldn't show up now, of course, no pack was in the mood for visitors a few days before the full moon. Ray should have told him sooner. But that was in the past, too. Right now, he couldn't hope to make anything better, just make sure it didn't get worse.

Alec sat them down to talk about what would happen if Ray went into heat.

"There's a chance it won't happen. The babies are still small, and they need Ray. But even if it does, one of us needs to be with them and make sure they don't do anything dangerous while..." He swallowed, then proceeded as diplomatically as possible, "Everybody else is busy."

Ray kept his eyes firmly on the grooves of the wooden floor. Even with the two pups currently sucking from his chest, it still took all of his willpower not to move. The angle was a little awkward, but they were able to keep their necks upright. And with their heads in the way, there was no part of Ray's swollen chest left exposed. He felt the alphas glance his way at Alec's casual reference to them fucking him. Holding his daughters kept him from hunching over, but he still had to tell himself off for the rush of humiliation their attention brought up. There was nothing to be embarrassed about, no matter how swollen his... his fucking *tits* were. It was natural, and it didn't matter if his chest had lost all hair and gone soft for the pups. It was what they needed, and Ray had no right to complain just because his body didn't look the way it used to.

He just couldn't imagine what it would feel like to be touched when he was like this.

"...but it's best not to knot him anyway," Alec was saying when Ray managed to calm down enough to listen again.

"But you are sure he won't conceive," Josh said, half a question in there.

"Pretty sure. It should come back gradually. First the sex, then... the rest."

"I don't get it," Josh insisted. "Aren't you an expert? How can you not know this?"

Alec snorted, "You think we study werewolves at med school, Josh? I'm guessing from the lore and what other werewolves have told me. Best we've got."

"Well, our best is crap," Iesu said rather mildly. He gave Alec his best charming smile. "No offence to you, mate."

The effects of the moon were multitude, but if you boiled it down to its essence, it made every instinct a shifter had come to the surface. Sometimes all at once. The basic three normally took precedence: eat, mate, protect the pack. It wasn't accidental that most werewolf attacks took place when the Goddess was in the sky; when you were moon-high, it was easy to interpret things as a threat to you and yours. And easier still not to think before you reacted to eliminate that threat.

Hunting was, of course, the whole reason they lived where they did—the idea of living near a city like Manchester sounded like a nightmare to Ray, much as he would have liked to visit—and usually happened first. Then there was mating... or sex, because unlike real wolves, the impulse was too entrenched into a werewolf's sexuality to be easily separated. During the full moon, if you were old enough and able-bodied enough, you'd end up tangled up with someone—your mate if you had one, a friend if you didn't. Ray remembered his first few full moons as a teenager as a little awkward, though he had never been really out of control—as his ability to stay away from other males had more than proven. He had ultimately done things he had been too shy to do sober. Nothing that made him uncomfortable come morning.

Until he became an omega. Suddenly, his body had developed instincts and needs Ray had never thought about himself; the wolf demanding it like it had once demanded a deer's blood or a drink of water. To be mounted, and bitten, and taken, and bred. If that wasn't bad enough, he wasn't affected by just his own wolf, but by the alphas' too: they had wanted to fuck him, and he had wanted it too. They had wanted to breed him, and he had wanted it too. He had found himself watching it happen, listening to them calling him a 'good boy' for spreading his legs like a good bitch, and not resisting as a knot stretched his insides to the point of pain. He had felt the heat of them coming inside him and known he was being bred, his wolf howling for joy. And he hadn't known what he wanted anymore.

He had let Josh kiss him and kissed him back, and tried his best to find his way back to the feeling he had had with the girls he had spent time with as a boy. The exhilaration and the rising excitement, the awkward tenderness of having someone expose themselves to you in the dark—all the soft, vulnerable parts of themselves open to your eyes and your hands and your mouth. He had looked at his friend and reminded himself that once upon a time he'd had to force his eyes away from his exposed skin.

And he had learned. Learned to accept what the wolf wanted, what the wolf made *him* want. Before, alphas had made him slightly wary of a fight. Now, their presence alone left him ready and wanting.

It wasn't completely new; he had looked at Sergi's mouth once, twisted in anger, and thought about licking the bloody lip he had just given him. But he had never thought about Sergi putting him on his knees and feeding him his cock, on sucking on it while Iesu entered him from the other end, making his growing belly bounce as he was fucked into from both ends.

He had learned to relax against Gabriel's wide arms, to feel safe when he was being held from behind, even when there was a hard cock pressed against his buttocks. Even when the hard cock was put inside his naturally lubricated entrance and he was fucked slowly and sweetly until a deep orgasm rolled through his body.

He still hated getting knotted outside of heat, but Gabriel only did it sometimes, when he couldn't help himself. And if he couldn't learn to like it, he had learned not to get angry; to let Gabriel lick him clean, and soothe him with food and pampering until he felt better.

They had all been very patient for the last three—almost four—months while Ray was too heavy for sex, and then while the babies were young and needy. After the first week, Ray had swallowed their come to keep the wolves quiet. They had fallen into a routine: he had knelt at their feet in their rooms at least a couple times a week—naked so his own orgasms didn't ruin his trousers and so his come would soak further into the house—and sucked them off or let them fuck his mouth. He had tried to time it so he only had to do them twice a week and he could relax the rest of the time, and they'd bravely kept their libidos in check except for those little breaks.

But he knew they had all been looking forward to heat. He wasn't stupid; they were looking forward to him being ready to breed again, too. He didn't think Josh's worry was false or faked at all, or that even Gabriel, as unsympathetic as he sometimes seemed, didn't care about what it would mean for Ray. But it was what their wolves needed. They could deny it all they liked—and even work to delay it with perfect honesty—but they couldn't stop wanting it.

Alec's advice was still on his mind: the lack of regular sex was surely making things even worse. He had been so busy hoping he wouldn't go into heat that he hadn't considered that healthy young men would want sex without the moon, and want it even more with it.

He'd been an idiot, of course, and now he had to hope he didn't go into heat. He needed to go back to bedding them without the moon if he had any hope they would be able to control themselves under its influence.

The first time they had taken him to a field during a full moon, Ray had been a virgin, still in shock from the revelation that he was starting his own pack. They'd tried their best, for alphas who hadn't had an omega before, but the sheer amount of sex, the heavy weight of the moon in his mind, and their overwhelming arousal had been enough for him to pass out. He didn't remember it clearly, but from what Alec had explained, he was pretty sure that, although they hadn't been able to restrain themselves to mounting him just once, they'd resisted the urge to knot him after the first time.

Now he was asking them not to do it at all. He was asking *Gabriel*, who sometimes did it involuntarily during normal sex. Even if it wasn't a breeding heat, it was a lot to ask. If it was... He would only have his own body's unwillingness to count on because after so long without, he didn't think he could count on their restraint this time.

They would try, he knew that. He could see their tenderness with the pups: the way Sergi made lists, and Iesu set up alarms to get to the store earlier for the fresh, soft rolls they were introducing them to. And nobody could miss how Josh had trouble making himself leave for his shifts at the gas station.

They would try, but all it'd take was one of them failing and the others would follow. An alpha in heat wouldn't be able to bear seeing his mate bred by another. If they lost control, they'd not be able to stop.

They wouldn't hurt him, not really, but Ray was a big man, and he didn't want to imagine how far his body would go if it was demanded of him. There was a saying about how even a single alpha could make his pack proud mounting a male omega... So, what could five do to him?

Chapter 2

"Gabriel," Ray said, and his cousin turned away from the view of the rolling green hills of their land. His eyes were almost the same colour when he blinked at Ray as if awakening from a daze. He had Maria's little body tucked against his neck, making him look large by comparison. Ray still remembered how big he'd seemed to him when he'd been young—now, they were practically of a height.

"You used to call me 'Gabi,'" Gabriel commented, leaning against the side of the house. He was rocking Maria to keep her calm. He didn't seem to mean anything by it, just a fond memory he was sharing with Ray.

Ray shrugged, feeling uncomfortable. He'd followed Gabriel around like he was a rock star as a kid. Gabriel had treated him like a little brother; teaching him to dribble, and teasing him about girls. And the moment Ray had presented omega, it was like it had never been. Like all the little gestures of companionship and care Gabriel had poured into their relationship meant nothing to him in the face of... He wasn't even sure of what. His cousin had said he was gay and that he had always liked Ray, and that was all. Like it was any kind of explanation. And Ray... he'd only had a few days to get used to the idea of being an omega, of needing an alpha, when he'd been presented with five.

He still wondered, especially with how... methodical Gabriel was when it came to bedding him. But it was too late to take it back, too late to ask. Ray didn't think he would like the answer anyway, and he didn't want to argue.

"I need a favour."

"Of course," Gabriel said at once. "Anything."

"I need you to make sure.... nobody knots." The words felt torn from his throat and he lowered his eyes without meaning to. He didn't know if it was him feeling shy or the wolf feeling submissive, but he couldn't seem to look up again even when Gabriel let the pause hold.

"We already spoke of this," Gabriel pointed out.

"Yes, but—" Ray shut his mouth. He didn't want to remind his cousin of his little 'accidents'; the ones nobody knew about because Gabriel didn't like to have the others around when he bedded Ray.

"You're worried because I did it when you weren't in heat," Gabriel said, voice carefully neutral.

Ray exhaled, shifting his weight. "I know you didn't mean to—"

"No," Gabriel said. "You are right." Ray looked up, surprised. "I didn't mean to, but it's still my responsibility. I should have looked after you better."

Ray shrugged. He wasn't looking for an apology. Gabriel had never done anything he understood would hurt Ray. He just didn't seem to understand Ray's reluctance. Most of the time, he seemed to think Ray was simply shy.

"So... you won't?" he checked.

Gabriel sighed. "I think we better make sure."

It took Ray a long moment to understand he was going to get fucked for the first time since giving birth. Gabriel didn't wait around for Ray to agree, he wasn't one to dither when something needed doing. He walked into the house ahead of Ray and stepped between Alec and the TV. Alec looked up but didn't object when he received a squirming Maria. "Is it the teeth? Maybe we can get to—"

Gabriel interrupted him like he always did; like he hadn't heard Alec speak. "We need some time alone," he explained, turning his body towards Ray. He glanced at Alec again with a thoughtful look. "You should probably see Ray later yourself; can't be too safe."

With that, he patted Alec's shoulder, careful not to jostle either Maria or her sister snuggled against Alec's other side and walked towards the bedrooms. Ray followed. At least Alec had the TV on. Ray could at least pretend that they wouldn't be overheard. It was possible to soundproof rooms well enough to give even werewolves privacy, but they didn't have the money for it yet.

Gabriel's room was at the end of the corridor. Like all the alphas' rooms, it was a little bare compared to Ray's and the babies'. Ray would have taken it anytime if it meant having his own space, but it just wasn't feasible while he was breastfeeding.

Gabriel wasn't the type to hang out in his bedroom unless it was for activities meant for such rooms, and Ray didn't have any reason to go in there on his own. When he was there to suck Gabriel off he normally kept his eyes closed. He hadn't noticed that Gabriel had put up a couple posters for the obscure Australian bands he liked. He hadn't had them up in his flat, even though it must have been at least three years since he'd moved out of his parents' place. Ray wondered if his cousin had never meant to stay there. He couldn't deny the untreated wooden floors gave the whole place a rustic look that suited Gabriel a lot better than the small, modern flat he'd moved into when Ray was a teenager.

He expected to be manhandled with the same decisiveness his cousin had shown in deciding this was happening, but Gabriel opened his arms in invitation and waited until Ray walked into them. He liked holding Ray to his body, and he was the only one of the alphas who was considerably bigger than him—the type of man whose size attracted attention wherever he went. He rubbed Ray's cheek and kissed his forehead, strangely... chaste.

Ray swallowed, suddenly nervous and Gabriel chuckled. "Come on, Raymond," he teased. "We know how to do this!"

Ray shivered. Most people only used his full name when they were mad at him, but Gabriel had always used it to tease him. He'd liked it. Coming from his worldly cousin, it had seemed like an acknowledgement of who he really was.

He'd admired Gabriel. A man who'd defied his parents and, to an extent, the pack: refusing to take a mate, moving into his own place, and spending his free time with his human co-workers. He didn't know what it meant now that Gabriel was no longer a rebel, and Ray was officially an adult but felt more out of control than ever.

"I know. It's just..." Ray shrugged, then leaned closer and returned the embrace, resting his face against Gabriel's chest. He didn't understand why he felt suddenly shy: Gabriel had seen every part of him, touched every part of him...

"Oh," Gabriel said in a small voice. "Is it this?" He slid a hand between them and cupped a palm around Ray's pectoral. Ray shuddered and tried to step back as he felt the soft flesh give a little as Gabriel lifted it off his chest. It wasn't much, in a guy that didn't have abs like Ray, it could just be fat. But it wasn't, and he bet fat didn't feel like that either, all tender and swollen, so sensitive that even such a little touch set him shivering. Gabriel had kept him close with his arm around Ray's waist, and now he swept his thumb across, barely grazing Ray's nipple through his shirt. Ray jumped like he had been electrocuted. Gabriel laughed. "Come to bed, honey, I want to *suck you*."

"I don't—" Ray started to say, breathless with Gabriel's lust and his own body's confused reactions; and then he was bouncing on the bed and Gabriel was standing between his half-spread legs.

"Ray, why do you insist on making everything hard?" he asked, sounding like an exasperated parent. "You like it, and why shouldn't you? It feels good, you just have to *let it*."

He didn't push Ray again, just waited patiently as Ray struggled to get over the strange feeling of wrongness the touch had brought out. It'd felt good, too, he couldn't deny that. Even if Gabriel could make him hard and slick just by thinking he wanted him, he'd never noticed the alphas being able to affect any other part of his body—not outside of heat. He raised a hand and put it around Gabriel's tanned forearm, then scooted back as he pulled. Gabriel went, crawling on top of Ray and slotting their bodies together. His folded knee was between

Ray's, pressing against Ray's swollen sack through his trousers. "We can... try it," Ray offered. He heard Gabriel's pulse spike in excitement.

"Okay," he whispered into Ray's ear and slid his hands into Ray's waistband to get his shirt off. Ray shivered as he was uncovered, not looking down at himself. But he didn't need to look, just hear the way Gabriel's breathing accelerated. He didn't understand why; Gabriel didn't find women attractive, why would he like that Ray—?

"Oh, god, you're beautiful," Gabriel murmured, reverent. He didn't touch Ray's chest. Instead, he placed his hands right under the curve of Ray's ribs and drew slow concentric circles downwards, a caress so slow it almost tickled. Ray found himself closing his eyes for a moment to feel it. Then Gabriel's hands moved down towards the newly flat planes of his belly, cupping the non-existent weight there. Ray had a flash of sense memory of being touched this way when he was full and heavy. He tensed, trying not to flinch or shiver. Gabriel chose to be safe and occupied his hands opening Ray's trousers instead.

He pushed Ray to lie back on the bed and knelt over him. When prompted, Ray raised his hips so Gabriel could remove his trousers and underwear. He pushed all of it off the side of the bed and stretched himself on top of Ray, heavy and hot, his clothes rough against Ray's naked skin. He tilted Ray's head back to lick at his throat, to seek his mark on Ray's neck—indelible and forever—and worried at it with his teeth as his hips started rolling against Ray's. Ray made a sound of distress when a button caught in his pubic hair, and Gabriel stopped cold, apologizing with a kiss to Ray's cheek. "Sorry, darling. Let me..."

Ray watched him get rid of his own clothes in a daze. He was tanned from work and big all over, and maybe he looked even bigger to Ray because he was standing over him, hard and about to mount him. Or maybe it was the omega's deep need to submit to his alpha. Ray didn't know where the feeling came from, but with Gabriel's heavy gaze on his exposed body, he knew what he looked like to his cousin. He had conveyed as much with his touch: his hands on Ray's hips and belly, possessive, proprietary, and his odd delight in Ray's tits swollen with pup milk. Gabriel thought they should do this so he wouldn't give into his urges during the full moon, but now that he wasn't <u>moon</u>-high, Ray could see what those urges were. Gabriel had never lied; he had told Ray he wanted to mate and breed him from the start.

He had also promised to protect and care for him. And this was what he needed to do to accomplish that, to get the fantasy out of his head and body so that he could be clear-headed when Ray would need it most.

Ray just had to let him. He let himself look at Gabriel's body, the healthy colour of his skin and the definition of his arms and chest. He'd grown even stronger in the last few years since Ray had seen him shirtless—since he'd moved out and started spending time in town outside of work. Ray hadn't wanted to notice any of it: not the muscles or the smile, and not his cousin's frequent absences. Or how he'd suddenly distanced himself from his pack to go hang out with humans.

But he had. And he had known that it was wrong.

And now he was simply supposed to accept it wasn't anymore. It wasn't okay for a fifteen-year-old beta to sigh after his grown-up male cousin, but it was expected of an omega to want his alpha. And nobody had a problem with the fact that it was the same person who was meant to feel both those things. Except for Ray. It was hard to have a man you'd dreamed of touching you for years look at you like you were perfect only when you no longer felt like yourself. *Because* you no longer felt like yourself.

He could have got a way worse deal than his teenage fantasy desperate for his body. But it was like a kick to the nuts... or somewhere a boy should have cared less about.

Heart racing, he made himself part his legs as Gabriel got back on the bed, shuddering when he pressed the length of their bodies together and getting a nice boost from Gabriel's own pleasure as he arched into him. Then his mouth was taken. It wasn't a kiss as much as an invasion, Gabriel's tongue and lips tasting every inch of Ray's mouth as if Ray was a space to be conquered. Ray made an effort to breathe through his nose, swallowing Gabriel's spit and his moans, feeling himself grow wetter as his alpha got more excited. Gabriel pulled back, groaning and rutting his hard cock against Ray's belly. He could smell that Ray was ready for him, and Ray expected his legs to be lifted. Not this time. Instead of bending Ray in half, Gabriel got to his knees and rolled Ray over onto his front. He lowered his own body onto Ray's, aiming his hard cock into the space between Ray's half spread legs. He moaned as his member touched Ray's soaked thighs, then thrust against him as he hitched his hips up until the head of his cock popped past the ring of muscle of Ray's arse. Ray shuddered, clenching in shock, and heard Gabriel murmur, "Oh, yeah, like that, I always—"

And then he was pushing in the rest of the way, pushing Ray's shoulders down while holding his hips in place, pinning him down as his cock breached further in. Deeper and deeper until it felt like one more inch would pierce him right through. Ray whimpered at the fullness, unable not to squirm at the feeling of having his arse used without any prep after four months. It didn't quite hurt, but it felt strange and uncomfortable. He had got used to not having this done to him.

Gabriel pulled out and pushed back in, deeper if it was even possible. Ray cried out as his cousin's cock pushed right against his prostate—and that set Gabriel off for real: rutting harder and faster into Ray as he held him down on the bedspread. He changed the angle that had set Ray's nerves tingling in his frenzy, but it didn't matter because soon enough he was coming, and Ray's own body rushed with his pleasure as his cock twitched and spilled untouched, forgotten in favour of the one emptying itself inside his body.

For a long moment, Gabriel panted against the side of his neck as they both tried to catch their breath, and then Ray felt a little pull inside. "Gabriel..." he begged. He could have physically pushed Gabriel off, but his wolf would never allow him to try and get away from his alpha mate. If Gabriel didn't react, Ray would have to lie there as the knot formed and then try not to cry in pain as it stretched inside him.

And he would do the same during heat, knowing all the while that a baby was probably being put inside him.

Gabriel swore and pulled out of Ray, fast enough to make Ray wince. He buried his face in the ruined sheets and breathed through the burning feeling the half-formed knot had left in his arse.

He felt the bed shifting and heard Gabriel's laboured breathing. It was taking too long for him to cool down, though. Ray twisted around to be able to see him. His alpha was sitting up, feet on the floor and face buried in his hands, back hunched in defeat. "What's wrong?" His voice came out rusty.

Gabriel exhaled and raised his head to look back at him. "You had to tell me," he explained. "That's not good enough. I can't need you to tell me, you won't be—"

He was right, of course. Ray would be in no state to ask for anything, not even something he truly needed.

"What if Alec asked?" he suggested weakly. Gabriel had clearly chosen Alec because he represented no threat, and Alec had given plenty of proof that he accepted his authority, but during the full moon they'd still be two alpha wolves who shared an omega. The last thing he wanted was to turn the tides of moon madness from sex to violence.

"No," Gabriel said. "Let me try again." For the first time, Ray thought he was really asking. If Ray refused, he wouldn't insist. It was like catching a glimpse of the man he'd known and admired. "I can do it, I just—it had been a long time. But I can do it now."

Ray shifted onto his side, feeling his arse complain even as it filled with more slick to allow him to fulfil his alpha's request. Gabriel must have been able to tell, but his eyes didn't leave Ray's face as he waited for an answer. Gabriel was right, it made sense that the first time after a long period of abstinence would be particularly intense and hard to control; that was the whole reason Alec had suggested he bed them before the full moon. It wasn't like Ray could honestly say he couldn't take it, not when he had lost his virginity to the five of them. He met Gabriel's eyes again. His cousin still looked soft and earnest. He nodded. "Okay."

The second time was sweeter, Gabriel didn't push as much as prod, guiding Ray where he wanted him on his back. But now that he had a clearer head, he had also remembered Ray's tits. His hands moved slowly from Ray's back to his chest, doubling down to brush against Ray's dick and then coming up back up again. It was just a detour, ultimately Ray knew their destination very well. He closed his eyes, the slow burn of Gabriel's arousal getting to him, but he opened them again as his alpha's hands once again cupped his pecs, caressing the flesh with his fingertips even as his palms lifted it a little as if assessing their weight.

Ray scrunched his eyes shut, the sensation so alien it felt like a foreign touch, and then he felt the wetness of breath. He startled. His back was against the wall behind the bed—there was nowhere to go.

"Gab—Gabi," he managed to rasp out.

Gabriel straightened, meeting his eyes with open concern. But Ray couldn't seem to find any more words. Not until Gabriel said, "Please tell me what's wrong."

"It doesn't... I don't, it's too weird."

His face fell. "Ray, I know it's new for you, but there's no reason for you to feel ashamed. I told you; you are beautiful."

"Why do you even like it?" Ray blurted out. "You don't like women. You don't like *breasts*."

The words doused the alpha's arousal noticeably enough that Ray felt his own body tense up. He was still a slick, wet mess, but he no longer felt empty.

Gabriel pulled away the hand he still had on Ray's hip and shifted until they weren't touching at all. "I like you, Ray."

"And *this* is me?"

His cousin hesitated, but then he nodded. "Yes. This is you."

"It's *not*," Ray bit back. Savagely furious, he yanked the blankets up to cover himself. "And you didn't want me," he added. An accusation, even though it was a ridiculous thing to accuse anybody of. Desire wasn't to be commanded, not by anything short of a natural force like the moon.

He knew at once that it was unfair, and looked up to apologize just in time to catch a flinch break through Gabriel's confusion. He closed his mouth, then opened it again. "Did you want me? Before I was an omega?"

He hadn't really thought about Gabriel's confession that he was gay when it'd happened because he'd been too busy freaking out about the five alphas he'd been assigned. But if he was... His cousin was uncharacteristically silent, gaze averted. Was his heart beating faster than before? Ray couldn't tell, he'd been too upset to pay attention. "Gabriel?" he pressed.

Gabriel exhaled, still not looking at Ray. "Okay, I suppose it does no harm to tell you now."

Ray waited, but nothing else seemed to be coming. "You did?"

"Yes," Gabriel bit out, looking sullen.

"I don't get it. What's the problem? I... I'm glad," Ray said. The admission didn't even feel like such a big deal in the face of Gabriel's obvious consternation.

"Ray, how old were you when you presented?"

"Eighteen."

Gabriel met his eyes, the intense, expectant gaze he'd used when Ray hadn't got the answer to his Maths problems. And then Ray saw what he meant: he had presented barely two months after his birthday, so if Gabriel had been interested in him before... Except that didn't sound like his rebellious cousin at all; worrying because he had a crush on someone a few months short of majority.

"So, you liked me before I could buy a pint, what's the big deal?"

"Raymond, I'm nine years older than you. It might not seem like a big deal now—"

"It was longer," Ray said. He met Gabriel's startled eyes. "How much longer?"

Gabriel gaped at him for a couple beats, then closed his mouth and looked away again. But then, once the question was asked, it was obvious. Gabriel had been a steady presence in his life until one day he'd informed his parents—who lived around the corner from Ray's own home—that he was moving into a flat at the very edge of town. It wasn't like alphas never left their pack, either to join another or to live in the human world for a while. Alec had been away at university for at least four years, maybe longer, and Nicholas and his friends had just up and left to find their fortune. But Gabriel hadn't really gone anywhere. He'd kept the same job, the same hours. He'd just exchanged his room at his parents' for a flat of his own a few miles away.

Close enough to the pack to visit but out of pack territory all the same. And he hadn't really visited, Ray knew that for certain because he'd asked Gabriel about it the next time he'd caught him on pack land. Gabriel had put him off with some line about being an adult and wanting to live like one.

Ray didn't remember if it had been a lie. He did remember why he'd asked, how betrayed he'd felt, how hurt despite knowing that Gabriel didn't owe him anything—definitely not anything as extreme as giving up his freedom to be close enough to hang out with him.

"Could you tell?" he asked quietly. He was naked in bed with a man who'd just fucked him. It didn't make him feel half as exposed as the memory of his teenage self demanding to know why he was being left behind.

Gabriel sighed, muscles glistening in the falling light as he shrugged. "That's why I had to move."

"But—"

"No," Gabriel him off. "You were a *child*. Don't even think..."

"You could have just told me. You didn't need to do anything about it."

Gabriel met his eyes. "It was the best I could do. I had to stay away from you, from... You wouldn't have done anything about it, not with all the homophobic bullshit they put into our heads. But I—"

"You wouldn't have," Ray said immediately. "You *didn't*."

Gabriel didn't seem comforted. "I still wanted to. And now..." He gestured between them. "I still want the wrong thing."

Ray's throat was closed up. He could think of words he wanted to say, but not a sentence. He leaned forward and took hold of Gabriel's wrist. He didn't know what he meant by the touch, but he wanted to give something back. "I thought it was because I was an omega."

Gabriel frowned at him, the same look that said, 'You're lucky I like you because you're an idiot'. It'd worked to make Ray rethink his answers when tested, and it worked now. "How was I supposed to know? You never even told us you were gay."

"I didn't tell you," Gabriel explained in a low voice.

"Me?" Ray repeated. "Who did you tell?"

"Josh knew. And Alec knew, too. We... Well, there's a club, not in town. In the city." Ray's hold on his arm slackened and he looked up. *Josh* knew, and even Alec—who Ray had never met before he'd become his omega—had been trusted to know. "I know you probably..." Gabriel continued. "I know it was probably hard for you, growing up without anybody to talk to about it. But I made Josh give me his word that he'd keep my secret, even from you."

"It doesn't sound like you liked me much." Ray let go of him and crossed his arms over his own blanket-covered knees. "It sounds like you wanted to fuck me."

"No!" Gabriel snapped. He reached for Ray, then forcefully closed his fist and pulled back. His come was drying on Ray's skin, but it was like speaking of this had brought him back to a point when touching Ray was not allowed. "I liked you, a lot. Enough that it scared the shit out of me. I didn't understand how I could feel that way for a kid. I just... I needed some space.

And if I had told you... Come on, Ray. The way you were... You were fifteen and clearly interested, how could I tell you I was gay without it being a come on?"

He thought back to Gabriel leaving from one day to the next, remembered dragging his eyes away from the naked skin of low riding trousers and not lingering when he patted well-formed arms. Toeing the line like he'd fall into a pit if he made one wrong move, only to wake up one day to discover it had all been for nothing. He hadn't hidden it well enough; the moon had seen through him. "Do you think you knew? That I was...?"

"An omega?" Gabriel guessed. "You weren't, though. You were a beta. That was the problem."

"That you had no excuse?"

"That you weren't *old enough*, Ray."

"And when I was, you didn't ask."

"Oh, give me a break!" Gabriel huffed. "It was two months, and I'd hardly talked to you for the last three years. Not to mention that the pack would have crucified me for it, if not both of us."

"I didn't think you cared about that," Ray accused. He knew he sounded childish, but maybe it couldn't be helped. After all, he *was* still nine years younger than Gabriel.

"I cared about you. I never stopped." It was the first time he'd talked about his feelings without sounding ashamed. Ray didn't know if he believed him. Could you really care for someone and not give them a choice?

"But you never..." He stopped, unsure.

"Never what?" Gabriel asked. He sounded tired, but eager too.

He wanted to know, Ray told the wolf. He made himself speak. "Ask."

"Ask what?"

Ray glared at the blankets under his clenched hands. "In bed."

Gabriel's breath audibly stuttered. "Ray—" His voice broke. "You... you like it. I..."

"I like to be asked," Ray said quietly.

"Fuck, I... Okay, I'll ask. Please stop me anytime I'm doing something you don't like." He hesitated, then his voice hardened. "That is an order. You must tell me."

Ray jerked in place. The wolf might not understand human language, but it knew that voice. "I don't like orders," he said at once, then glanced up at Gabriel in surprise. It was his cousin's damn fault if he didn't like it.

Gabriel sighed. "I keep fucking up, don't I? I take it back. It's not an order. But I would really like it if you told me. It would... It would help me take better care of you if you told me."

"I don't know if I can, not when..."

"Heat?"

Ray nodded.

"You can tell me after, though. Right? And before?"

"Yeah," Ray agreed, reluctant not because he didn't want to, but because Gabriel's attitude seemed to have shifted so suddenly he didn't quite know how to take it. But if his cousin had been telling the truth, if he'd really left pack territory to get away from Ray... Maybe he'd been angry. It wasn't fair. Just like Ray's own resentment at being abandoned wasn't fair. But he could understand how lonely Gabriel must have felt with a secret like that. Not just that he was attracted to men, which a lot of pack members could have sympathized with, but that he wanted to sleep with someone so much younger than him.

"Good," Gabriel said. He licked his lips. "Would it feel good if I fucked you now?"

Ray straightened, staring. Gabriel wasn't hard; his cock was pink and pliant against his thigh. For once, he wasn't taking Ray's arousal for granted. Even though Ray's arousal *was* guaranteed. He could make Ray react any time he liked, but he was asking instead. "I... Have you heard of foreplay?" he asked, trying for teasing. His voice was a mess, too nervous, too awkward, but Gabriel smiled.

"Here and there." He extended a hand to Ray, palm up. "What about kissing? Can I kiss you, Ray?" he asked, not once looking away.

Ray couldn't look away, either, trapped in the blue of his eyes, hooked on the softness of his smile. He took the hand offered and pulled, forcing Gabriel to scramble to balance on his knees in front of Ray. And then he kissed him; raised his face and licked at his lips. Asking. Gabriel opened up at once, letting Ray lick into his mouth. It was a kiss as different as any they'd shared so far as the same act could possibly be. Even when Gabriel's tongue dipped into Ray's mouth to explore, he was giving, not taking.

Ray put his hands on Gabriel's shoulders, let his fingers curve over the strength of them. Gabriel's breath caught in their kiss, and, encouraged, Ray squeezed. A shudder ran through his lover. He cupped Ray's face with his hands, tilting his face slightly for the kiss as Ray's hands explored first his back, then the dip of his waist. It was no wonder Ray hadn't been able to look past his body when he'd been a kid—he was like something carved out of a dream.

Gabriel turned his face aside, breathing heavily. Ray could smell his arousal. He was hard. So was Ray. He didn't need to wonder why, though. He slid his hands further down, to the curve of Gabriel's magnificent arse—and then he pulled him forward against his own body. Gabriel made a sound surprisingly close to a whimper when his cock met Ray's half-blanketed body.

Ray cursed, low and annoyed, then pushed Gabriel back. Gabriel stiffened for half an instant—probably feeling Ray was jerking him around—then leaned back far enough to let Ray push the covers down. His eyes flickered down Ray's chest at once but didn't stop until they reached Ray's lap. He glanced up, a question on his face.

"Enough foreplay," Ray told him, beckoning.

Gabriel still hesitated. "Do you want...?"

To get fucked. Even though his alpha had not said the words, he must have been thinking about it because Ray felt himself grow wet. Gabriel inhaled and shivered, but didn't move.

"We should," Ray said. It was the truth. "To be safe."

Gabriel's posture was tense, but he nodded. He knew Ray was right. It didn't matter that they'd talked things over; there were things that were still beyond their control. But even though they were headed the same way they had been so many times, when he reached for Ray this time, it was different. Maybe it was the shared knowledge. Ray didn't know, but the same hands that had held him down were now barely touching him. Ray leaned back of his own accord and Gabriel followed, kissing his throat as his hands ran down Ray's body. His sides and his hips, but not his upper chest. Ray felt his eyes close as he shivered. Then the touch stopped. He opened his eyes and found Gabriel looking at him. Waiting. "I want..."

Ray made an inquiring noise. It was true that the wolf would probably make him want to do it, but that didn't matter; he wanted to do it already. Gabriel licked his lips. "Could you touch me? So I know—"

Ray smiled, then pulled him back down so that his body covered Ray's completely. Their hips jerked when their dicks brushed together, and Ray let out a strangled laugh, half pleasure, half surprise. "I know I did this to myself, asking for foreplay. But I didn't mean we should go from supersonic to snail-paced."

Gabriel raised his head to give him an unimpressed look, then got a hand between their bodies and took hold of Ray's cock. Hard and sure, a man's expert grip. Ray swallowed, fighting to keep his eyes from closing as he trembled. Gabriel slid his hand down to the head, spreading the wetness there along the length of Ray's erection torturously slow before he started jerking him off in earnest. Ray's hips followed the touch, thrusting hard into the warm grip even as he buried his hand in Gabriel's hair and smashed their mouths together in a kiss that was more spit than tenderness. Gabriel gave as good as he got, his own erection dragging against Ray's hip.

Ray's left hand tightened on Gabriel's side. "I... Stop, I'll come!"

Gabriel laughed, a pleased rumble Ray felt reverberate through his own chest. "That was the idea, darling."

"Ray," he corrected, emboldened by their confessions or the joy in Gabriel's face. They were lying on their sides. His cousin was propped on his elbow, watching his face as he touched him.

"Ray," he echoed, and twisted his grip, thumb pressing against the swollen head of Ray's dick. "Come for me."

And Ray did. Helplessly and dizzyingly hard. He clutched at Gabriel as he tensed, hard enough that when his vision cleared he could smell blood.

He tensed, but Gabriel shushed him. "Love bite," he said. "It'll heal as soon as you let go."

Ray snatched his hands away. His fingers felt stiff with how hard he'd been holding on. He tilted his head to check on Gabriel's upper arm. The marks of his nails were already red lines, but he'd smeared a little blood as he'd pulled away. It looked strangely beautiful against Gabriel's skin, he thought, maybe a little dazed still by the force of his orgasm. "You can, you know," his cousin said, and Ray glanced up at his face. Gabriel didn't clarify, but he licked his reddened lips. Slowly. And Ray realised he was doing the same. He wanted... "Maybe there's some things we can't choose, but this is yours, if you want it."

Ray glanced away, feeling suddenly exposed. This was nothing to his naked body under Gabriel's, cock softening and come splattered all over both their bellies. But it didn't feel like nothing. He hadn't even known he wanted something like that, and he didn't... He swallowed, shook his head. "Let's..."

Gabriel paused, and Ray thought that he might be disappointed, but he didn't look at his face to find out. He placed a gentle kiss on the corner of Ray's jaw. "Do you want to turn around?" he offered. His fingers already sliding down slowly from Ray's hip to the curve of his arse.

Ray didn't say anything, just rolled away onto his other side. Gabriel understood, curling up behind him, close but without the overwhelming intimacy of looking each other in the eye. And then he stopped. "I need you to tell me. I don't want..."

And he was right, of course. Ray had told him to ask. He was asking. It was hard to answer, though. It was hard to talk about it. He bent his elbow and reached back for Gabriel's closest hand, placing it between his own legs where he was wet and still a little tender from their first round. Gabriel pushed a finger in—just the one—and Ray clenched around it. He wanted more. Or maybe he needed it. It was hard to tell anymore. He thought Gabriel must have known, but maybe he just assumed it was his own desire and not Ray's because he was slowly sliding his thumb against Ray's rim, making him shiver. Ray breathed through it, trying not to rush him as he pushed a second finger in slowly when none were really needed. Gabriel scissored his fingers and Ray shifted his hips, unable to stand the exposure for long. Gabriel's thumb pushed into the mess of slick and come behind his balls. He arched into it, feeling empty despite the slight soreness, and Gabriel made a pleased sound before pushing his fingers deeper into Ray. Ray clenched around them, heart pounding. Gabriel kissed his neck, he was straining with the effort to stay still behind Ray. He asked.

"Yes," Ray replied, helpless to resist. "Yes, do it."

Gabriel still didn't rush, pulling his fingers out and lining his cock with an almost insulting calm. Ray couldn't stand the wet, gaping emptiness anymore. As soon as he felt the head poised to enter him, snapped his own hips back to receive it. He messed up the angle, though, and instead of going into him, Gabriel's cock slid wetly against his balls. Gabriel gasped against Ray's shoulder. "Fuck, Ray..." he panted, pushing his cock into the space between Ray's buttocks like he couldn't stop the reflex. Ray whimpered at the feeling: the wonderful silkiness of Gabriel's dick against the delicate skin of his balls and hole and the terrible emptiness he felt when he clenched around nothing. He was so close to getting what he truly needed...

Then Gabriel was taking hold of his hips and lining himself up. He gave a good push that got his cock to pop past the ring of muscle again. The moment he was inside Ray, Gabriel leaned in close, arm going around his waist. Ray could feel his heart beating wildly against his back. Ray squirmed, trying to get him to move as the sensation of Gabriel's cock breaching him deeper sent a shock of pleasure through his whole body. He clenched around the heavy weight inside. "Ready?"

Ray grunted in response, putting a hand down on the bedding to get enough leverage to thrust back onto his lover's cock. Gabriel let out a sound like he'd been hit hard on the solar plexus, and his hips snapped into the movement. Just like that, they were fucking. It was a hard angle for both of them and it wasn't enough, but Gabriel seemed determined to stay in that position.

"*Just fuck me*," Ray snapped, reaching back and digging his nails into Gabriel's hip to yank him close. Gabriel made a choked noise in his ear, but complied, pushing Ray face down into the bedding and giving it to him hard and fast. Ray sagged for a moment, the relief so intense it left him weak. But he needed to come too badly too just lie there, so he got a knee under his body and pushed back.

Gabriel immediately helped him raise his hips, never letting his cock leave Ray's hole completely but slowing down enough long enough for Ray to get on his hands and knees. And then it was perfect. It didn't take long—Gabriel was desperate after having made Ray come without finishing himself—and Ray felt like he hadn't had real sex for so long, he'd explode. He *wanted* it. Not reluctantly, not because the wolf made him, or because Gabriel did, but because it was his body and Gabriel's fat dick was hitting him in the perfect spot with every thrust. And then Gabriel did something he'd never done before; he reached around and closed his hand around Ray's cock and *pulled*. Ray screamed, pleasure flooding over him, too much at once for his nerves to handle. And then he was coming, clenching hard around the cock buried deep in him. And Gabriel was coming, too. The orgasms rolled into one another, Ray's barely starting to fade when Gabriel's peaked, forcing Ray's body into another wave of ecstasy.

He must have dozed off afterwards. Not too long, Gabriel was no longer inside him, but the sting still hadn't quite faded when he felt his cousin pressing close again, curling his body against Ray's back and cocooning him in his warmth.

"Told you," Gabriel said. He didn't sound smug, though, just relieved.

He hadn't knotted, Ray realised. He'd completely forgotten about it. He reached back and patted Gabriel's thigh. His cousin laughed, maybe because he had literally fucked Ray out of words. He reached over Ray's prone body and dragged the blanket over them both, and then there was nothing to keep Ray awake anymore.

Chapter 3

Alec knocked on Ray's door as soon as he got home. Ray wasn't surprised, but he was drained. He'd had a full night sleep for the first time in maybe a week—not the five hours he'd been getting between feedings—and woken up with Gabriel's alarm. His nipples had been killing him, tits too full after so many hours. He'd bolted before Gabriel had woken up enough to try to talk to him. The babies had been fine—the others must have fed them something else, maybe that enhanced formula Alec had decided would be better than having them drink fresh cow milk—but Jamie had happily latched on when Ray had sat with him.

He didn't mind breastfeeding so much, especially compared to being pregnant. He'd spent the day with the pups—for once relieved that they couldn't communicate beyond whimpers and yips. But time was running out, and now he had to face the music.

"Um, so you decided to go for prevention?" Alec asked, still in his doorway.

Ray nodded. "Yes." After his conversation with Gabriel, he felt like he'd run out of words. He glanced back at the babies sleeping on his bed and Alec blushed. "Is Josh awake?"

The TV had been on in the living room for a while, but Josh had come back from his night shift at eight that morning and hadn't slept, and Iesu and Sergi wouldn't be back for at least an hour.

"Yeah, he had like three Red Bulls at work. Even though they're terrible for you," Alec babbled.

Ray hesitated. Would it be enough to leave the door of his bedroom open? The railings were up, so even if the babies rolled over in their sleep, they wouldn't fall. He had no hope in hell that the others wouldn't know what he had done with Gabriel. Not even if he wasn't about to do it with Alec, who still blushed around Ray and couldn't have kept it a secret from noseless humans. But the idea of going over there and *announcing it...* He couldn't do it.

He was happy to have talked things through with Gabriel, more than, really. But he didn't have the energy to do it again so soon. And enjoyable as the sex had been, he didn't really want to be that close to anyone again either.

It'd been too long, obviously. He shouldn't have allowed himself to believe he could decide for himself what kinds of sex he had. Or when. He needed to stop hoping that, somehow, he could twist his circumstances so that his body would belong to him again. The period after giving birth had been an illusion, an exception, not what Ray's life was really like.

Alec put a soft hand on his hip, then offered quietly, "I'll tell Josh to keep an ear open for them. He might even prefer to come nap with them than watch TV. Even if only to watch them like a total dope."

Ray gave him a weak smile. They all thought Josh's baby craze was sweet, but he was too discomfited to truly return the smile. He went to Alec's room to wait and took off his clothes. It was a little selfish to try and speed things along, but he hoped Alec wouldn't mind.

Alec gasped when he saw him, and they were tangled together in the bed a moment later. Alec's mouth was on his, greedy and overwhelming. Ray kissed him back. He got wet for him. Then his legs were lifted and hooked over Alec's shoulders. He tilted his head away from his kiss to breathe out slowly as Alec lined up his dick with Ray's hole and pushed it in. He shuddered as he bottomed out, and Ray concentrated and relaxed his inner muscles for him, letting him pull out and push in again a few times before his hips started pistoning in and out of Ray faster and faster, making Ray's cock bob madly between them.

It was over pretty quick, after all, but Ray let Alec hold him afterwards and hoped that made up for it.

The knock woke him from a light doze. Alec was gone, but the two heartbeats outside the door made it clear he hadn't simply remembered he had left something in the oven. Alec was his doctor and he had taken it upon himself to administer Ray's course of treatment: he had told the others. He sat up, pulling the sheets as he went to remain at least covered enough for decency.

If he didn't answer, they'd probably go away. But he had seen the effects of Alec's advice before: an alpha who'd had sex with him outside of heat had a much easier time being careful when the moon was pulling at him.

"Come in," he called out, only realising he was in Alec's room when Iesu had already opened the door. Sergi met his eyes from the doorway, his own expression guarded. Ray was about to get up and offer to go to their room when Iesu shoved Sergi in with an impatient sound and closed the door unhurriedly behind himself. Ray supposed there wasn't much of a point in covering up either; it wasn't like anybody there hadn't seen Ray naked plenty of times.

Iesu turned to Ray with a sunny smile, but with Iesu, it was hard to say if it meant he was particularly happy. It might be leftover amusement from catching his favourite cartoons or one of the babies doing something cute.

"Hey, Ray," he said, perching on Alec's chair in a way Ray was pretty sure Alec wouldn't have approved of. Ray hoped Clara got that uncanny ability to be happy at the smallest things. "Alec said you'd got over that headache of yours, honey."

Ray laughed, surprised. From the doorway, Sergi snorted.

"More like had a whole box of aspirin," he explained, not completely sure what he was saying, but Iesu smiled at his attempt anyway.

"Do you want me to go?" Sergi asked. Ray turned to look at him in surprise. They'd never asked him before if it bothered him that they were lovers, or that they preferred to have sex with him together. Sergi shrugged. "I guess... it's been a while. I don't know how you feel about... anything, really. But I could come back later, or in the morning."

"We could both come back in the morning," Iesu added, a little more careful, but nowhere near as serious as Sergi.

"But... don't you have work?" Ray checked.

Iesu shook his head. "Day off, all of us. Except Gabriel, who is a masochist, says he doesn't mind working the day of the full moon."

They let Ray think it over for a minute while they made fun of Gabriel's work ethics. Ray couldn't see why not. He was still quite sore from Gabriel and Alec and the closer they were to the full moon when they did it, the better it had to be. He looked up at them. "Tomorrow sounds nice."

Iesu clapped his hands together and jumped to his feet like, for some unfathomable reason, he was pleased that Ray had asked to delay having sex with him. "Okay, so now, what about a movie marathon? We'd have to start with something PG because it's only six and, man, you make truly energetic babies! But we can move on to something a little meatier later. You in?"

Ray stared at him. "*I* make energetic babies? Have you seen yourself? You've been working all day and you're chipper than a bird at sunrise."

At this, Sergi burst out laughing. "Oh, god, that's so true."

"Whatever," Iesu sing-songed. "You guys are just jealous. Do you want popcorn?" he asked Sergi, then turned to Ray. "I don't know how I don't know this, but do you like yours salty or sweet?"

"Skipped the movie dates," Ray said easily. "And I don't like popcorn. I'll take M&Ms if there's any."

I t had taken a while to convince Iesu that nothing was wrong with Ray for disliking inflated cereal, but in the end, they'd found some crisps in the cupboard and made hot chocolate to share and settled in the living room. Josh was there, half covered in sleepy babies and keeping an eye on Clara and Sasha's multi-coloured block project on the floor in front of the TV.

The TV was off, so their kids had been Josh's sole source of entertainment until Iesu walked in and selected a child-friendly DVD. It wasn't surprising that Josh didn't look that alert himself, but he smiled when he saw them come in. Maria and Michael were resting against his sides, carefully cradled in his arms. Jamie was lodged between his shoulder and the couch in a way that a baby four months old could have never accomplished—clearly, their son had got there on four paws and then changed back. At least he still had his diaper on, Ray supposed. Changing diapers with an enhanced sense of smell was never going to be fun, but it was even less so when the babies in question could get out of their diapers by simply changing into pups and back again.

Tossing Sergi the remote, Iesu swooped up Clara and Sasha both and twirled them around. They squealed their delight before he settled them all into the other two-seater. He gave Sergi and Ray an expectant look. "Come on, movie's going to start."

Sergi rolled his eyes at him, walking closer. "It's Lilo and Stitch, Iesu."

"So?" Iesu replied, face blank, then noticed Ray was still standing. "Maybe unearth some of your boy's limbs before you squeeze in there, Ray," he suggested, and Ray froze for a second, his heart speeding up.

But Iesu was in too a good mood to allow any awkwardness. He met Ray's eyes and tilted his head towards Sergi, silently indicating the way they were pressed close together and shrugging. Ray turned towards Josh—who didn't seem to have heard—and collected Jamie to a grateful groan from his friend.

"Oh, god, I think he broke me," Josh said, moving his neck side to side to relieve some of the tension. Jamie snuffled unhappily until he realised whose arms he was in, then nuzzled his face against Ray's collarbone, hungry even in his sleep. Ray ignored the way his shirt was getting wet with spit and shot Josh a questioning look.

"Mikey," Josh requested. He was rumpled and a little sleepy himself, Ray saw, and the baby in question probably was quite heavy to have lying on your arm for hours on end. He put Jamie down on the other end of the sofa, where his son blinked lazily awake, and snagged Michael up from his father, surprised still by the difference in size between them. Not that any of them were truly small—Alec thought their growth rate at this stage was twice as fast as that of human babies—but Jamie was still a good pound heavier than the others.

Ray turned Jamie around and sat with him on his lap just in time for the credits, ignoring Josh's fussing over Maria, and Sasha's giggles as Iesu gave into the temptation to tickle her. He was about to shush him when Sergi got there first. Ray didn't catch what he said, but it worked like a charm, getting

Iesu to hold the baby against his chest without any further shenanigans. His eyes snagged on the way they all looked together: Sergi's head patiently tilted to listen to Iesu's probably in-depth explanations about how the film had been made, and the way Sasha was sprawled all over Iesu's lap like she was a queen on her throne while Clara was ignoring the movie; too intent on the buttons on Sergi's checked shirt.

They looked like a family.

And then Josh got up to get the popcorn bowl closer and blocked his view. His friend, Maria safely tucked into his side but awake now, was turning his way with a steaming mug of hot chocolate from the carafe Sergi had set up well out of the babies' reach.

"Put them down," he said, gesturing towards the couch, and Ray did, arranging Jamie and Mikey in a sitting position to watch the TV, where the tiny alien had gone from looking cute to murderous in an instant. Josh deposited the mug in Ray's cupped palms with a satisfied smile. The brush of his fingers against Ray's skin made him shiver.

"You're looking thin these days," he said with the thick northern accent he had learned from imitating his Mancunian grandfather. He'd hoped Josh hadn't heard Iesu's teasing, but he knew him too well to mistake the awkward joking for anything but discomfort.

Ray shot him an unimpressed glare and sipped, sitting back down on the arm of the sofa so he could watch both the TV and his sons. Iesu had called Josh 'his boy', but that was too simplistic. If Josh felt something other than friendship and attraction for him, he had never said so. And Ray... Well, what did it matter what Ray felt for him? Josh was his mate, and so were the other four. Ray had a responsibility to them. He could talk to Gabriel about how he'd felt when he'd been a kid. Three whole years ago. It didn't need to mean anything for the present. Gabriel didn't... if his interest had ever been romantic as well as sexual, it was long over now. Ray's old crush wasn't going to make anybody feel left out. But Josh wasn't his past. Josh had never left. Ray had never stopped... It was all fine and dandy for Iesu and Sergi to play boyfriends, but Ray didn't fool himself that his alphas would take it well if he showed a marked preference for any of them. They understood Josh had been his best friend all his life, and that he'd known Gabriel the longest. But anything beyond that...

It would be foolish to imagine that, because he was theirs, it meant they were his.

But Iesu wouldn't just let it go. He had seen something on Ray's face the day before when he had made that comment, or maybe he had made that comment because he had seen something. Whatever it was, he couldn't resist making a point of it, not even seeming to notice how odd it was to try and talk about Ray's feelings for another man when his come was still leaking from Ray's arse.

Ray tensed, but even in the large king beds all the alphas had in their rooms, he didn't really have far to go with Iesu behind and Sergi in front of him. Sergi's eyes blinked open—sex made them all much more acutely aware of the others' bodies, and Ray had heard his own heart rate spike. He hoped Sergi would understand, or at least be more willing to respect Ray's desire to avoid the topic, but his ex-rival gave him a sad smile.

"Would it be so bad to try?" he asked, and Ray found the strength to sit up despite his wolf's profound dislike for the idea. He was pretty sure he could get off the bed, too, but he was already feeling a little shaky. He turned to face them both and glared instead.

"Would... Oh, of course, what's a breakup or a rejection from someone *you can never walk away from*?" he spat.

Iesu followed him up, raising his hands at the same time as he got upright, like his abdominal muscles allowed him to move in any direction he liked independently of gravity. He wisely didn't try to move from his position next to the headrest, though. "Okay, let's look at who is saying this to you." He pointed at Sergi.

Ray snorted. "And you want me to believe it's the same thing?"

"Yes, we bonded, that means we cannot leave," Iesu said simply.

"It does mean you can make yourself a house down the road and come visit me," Ray pointed out. "It *does* mean you don't have to keep sleeping with him." Ray had known he was right, but watching Iesu's expression crumble didn't give him any satisfaction. He let himself lower his eyes to concentrate on keeping his breathing even.

He felt a tentative hand on his arm, just fingertips patiently waiting for their welcome. He froze, angry and sad, and so *fucking lonely*. He knew he was right; he'd known all along... but he wanted what they had. More than anything. Maybe even more than freedom. But it was a catch-22 because freedom was what you needed for real love. To choose someone, you had to be able not to choose them.

He hadn't chosen them, not really. But he could choose this much, he could take the comfort they offered. He turned into Sergi's body, felt his strong arms surrounding him, supporting him, as he sobbed. He had lost control of his breathing from one exhalation to the next and now he was shaking, tears running down his face and into the bare skin of Sergi's shoulder. His alpha didn't react at all, like he couldn't even feel it. He just held Ray firm, a solid point in a world that wouldn't stop changing, where the foundations of his life crumbled like primary school art projects and nobody seemed to *understand...*

At some point, Iesu got him some tissue, and later, when Ray could breathe enough to drink it, water. He had got another bunch to clean up Sergi, who didn't even look his way as his lover dried the mess Ray hoped was only tears. Ray remembered Sergi's ability to focus from when they'd been boys intent on getting the other to concede defeat over every little thing. Now there was no anger in the alpha's expression, but it was even more intimidating to be looked at that closely in concern. Sergi was really *looking* at him, not at some built-up image of who he was.

"I didn't realise," he said. Ray shrugged. He didn't have the energy to tell him that he hadn't realised what it meant to be an omega before he had become one. But Sergi continued, "That you were this unhappy. I thought... the pregnancy was hard for you, that you were scared of what your body could do. And I got that, as much as I can, because it's miraculous, but if it was happening to me..."

Ray looked up in surprise. He wanted to speak, in anger perhaps. *How could anybody not realise?* He still remembered the first months after he had been given to them: the sheer bleakness of his first time, the deep dragging knowledge of the babies inside him...

"I thought you were better," Iesu said, dispirited, from where he was standing beside the bed. "You've been laughing more since the babies were born; you don't even seem to mind if we see you breastfeed them now."

Ray flinched at the word, too worn-down to hide it now. And what was the point anyway? Hiding his pain had got him into this mess in the first place. Iesu made a small, hurt noise. Ray kept his gaze away from him, not wanting to see the pity on his face, having enough with his own pain.

"You do mind," Iesu said. "Why would—?"

Ray sighed. "I knew this was coming."

"This?" Sergi asked. "Sex?"

"Yes. Hard to... can't really have it dressed."

"So, you've been letting us see you like that because..." Iesu said in a strangled voice.

Ray shrugged, consciously trying not to hunch over to hide his chest. "It's my life, Iesu, I've got to get used to it."

"Get used to it?" Iesu repeated. "You don't have to get used to us! If you don't like something—"

Ray sighed, heavily. "You can't possibly believe that. Do the maths. Let's say everything goes well; I've got... two more months before I go into heat, eight months until I..." The words dried in his mouth, but he made himself finish the sentence. "Till we have another litter."

That gave Iesu enough of a pause that Ray glanced up at him. He looked stunned for a long moment, then he spoke, "So what? If you don't want us to look, we won't."

Ray thought about Gabriel doing a lot more than looking. It'd felt good. Physically. He was grateful to Gabriel for stopping, but he also couldn't help but feel like he'd done something wrong. He should have wanted it. He could want it; he only had to grit his teeth long enough for it to stop feeling so wrong. Once, getting fucked had felt like that. And now he had just had these two men inside him and he was managing a very intense conversation with them. He had enjoyed it; he'd *learned* to enjoy it. That was the life he wanted, not one he had to suffer through.

"I don't think that's a good idea," he tried to explain. "I don't want... some things are going to be too... They're going to keep happening, for a long time. If I'm afraid of everything... I don't think I can live like that."

He didn't need to look at Iesu to know he'd lost all traces of his usual smile. "So, you're just going to grit your teeth and... what? Think of England?"

Ray met his alpha's eyes with open defiance, too angry to be pulled back by the wolf. "Yes," he said. "I will grit my teeth until I get used to it, and then it'll stop being a big deal. That's how life works, Iesu, and I don't have time for idealism."

"You are going to say yes to them," Sergi said suddenly, voice full of anger and horror.

Ray startled, turning to him, suddenly unsure, but then he remembered what he had just said. "I will do what I have to do."

"You don't have to do that," Sergi insisted, leaning forward to take hold of Ray's wrist.

Ray froze, but he didn't think Sergi knew it for what it was: the omega wolf reacting to its alpha. It wasn't an actual demand, thankfully, so with an effort, Ray could talk again. He hesitated, but foolish as it was, he didn't want to undermine their efforts. "I'll tell you the same thing I told Josh; find me a solution that gets more adults into the pack without it."

He clenched his fist until his nails dug into his palm, using the pain to pull away from the lulling effects of Sergi's touch. To his surprise, Sergi's hold loosened as he turned to Iesu. Ray caught the look their shared out of the corner of his eye, but couldn't interpret it. "What?"

"Well," Sergi said. "If you are looking for a guy that can charm people into wanting to be in our tiny pack without asking for a lot..."

Ray looked at Iesu, too. "What does he mean?"

Iesu's eyes were darker than ever. "He means we will try," he replied, and Ray didn't need a map to understand that Iesu didn't want to tell *him* what the plan was, for whatever reason. He had never seen him so far from a smile before, but he'd never seen him try and solve a serious problem before. He didn't want to hope, but his heart stuttered anyway.

Chapter 4

R ay had left them to it and gone in search of Josh, firmly keeping his mind on the corridor he was traversing and the possible ways to decorate it to make it look like a home before the kids started noticing those sorts of things. He'd have to talk to his mum about it. Despite how little money there had always been to go around, their place looked cosy.

He found Josh in his own room, lying on the bed and getting his hair played with—read: pulled—by Maria's tiny hands as he lay on his side, facing the door. Ray wondered if Josh had been expecting him. If he had, he'd got distracted in the meantime because it took him a moment to look up from where he was petting Jamie's light brown fur. It'd only been about a month since the babies had figured out they could control their own shifting, and at the beginning, if one of them shifted, the others had tended to follow—but not anymore. They were becoming their own people, Ray realised, heart squeezing at the thought. He could barely stomach the idea of them not needing him around all the time, even if part of him longed for the freedom.

Josh's face brightened from his casual smile into true pleasure at the sight of Ray, like... He had seen that before, he could admit that, it didn't hurt anything to admit that. But that being true didn't make anything else possible, not as things stood. He shook himself out of it and blocked the door with his foot to keep Sasha inside before crouching to pick her up. She shifted back into a baby, and he had to scramble to get a hold on her as Josh laughed from the bed—beautifully lazy and completely entrancing. With his daughter secured, Ray raised his eyes to his friend.

"Did Alec...?" he asked, trailing off in hopes he wouldn't need to say more.

Josh looked at him blankly for such a long moment that Ray thought he would have to ask. Then his face flushed, his eyes widened, and he straightened up so fast Maria lost her hold and fell back on the bed. Josh was ready to catch her, turning his upper body around without disturbing the sleeping boy next to him, and she ended up laughing when she bounced on the mattress. After checking she was not going to roll off in a fit of hilarity, he turned to Ray.

"Ray..." he breathed out the name like it was a spell.

Ray looked down at Sasha's dark hair, rubbing her back to keep her from squirming. "We can go to your room," he offered. It was probably best, anyway, since the babies had grown used to napping on the huge bed in his own bedroom.

"I—Should we get... I don't know, Alec?"

Ray cursed himself, silently but viciously. *Why hadn't he asked someone else to come over?* He shook his head and pulled out his phone. He hesitated for a moment, then texted Iesu with his free hand. Sasha tried to cling to him when he put her down on the bed, as if she could sense his distress.

"No, stay," Ray said firmly and straightened. Josh sneaked a hand between them and tickled her, distracting her long enough for Ray to take a step back.

"I'll come to you in a bit," he told Ray, not looking up from the giggling babies. Ray didn't even answer before he got out of there. He met Iesu at the door, but the alpha just nodded and walked around him.

Ray considered undressing, but if he had felt uncomfortable about the others seeing his chest, it'd be even worse with Josh. Josh wouldn't push or even mention it. Hell, Josh must have needed Ray as badly as the others—if not worse since it'd been longer—and he had never let it show at all.

He couldn't help but wonder where Josh's self-control came from. He'd been the first to offer to mate Ray, after all, so it couldn't be lack of interest, could it? But, of course, it was easy for an alpha to be interested in an unmated omega; all that was needed was the most basic of mating instincts. That was why sexual orientation was not considered a problem when it came to male omegas. You didn't need to have any interest in males the rest of the time to want an omega in heat, and afterwards... Ray knew how alphas justified it: male omegas weren't really men anymore, not when they were bred, when their bodies softened with the curves of pregnancy and breastfeeding, when they submitted just like a woman would. Nobody had ever used the word 'bitch' to talk about him, but they didn't need to.

It was a bad line of thought to have right before Josh came to fuck him for the first time in months, but Ray couldn't help it. He needed to know if everything that Josh did for him, *to* him, was just an alpha's instincts.

It shouldn't have mattered. But, of course, it did; he hadn't really wanted to get fucked by any of the alphas. Not in the circumstances in which it'd happened. But if he had any hope of forging something real—whether a sexual relationship or anything else—he needed to know. Talking to Gabriel had hurt. It seemed like some cosmic joke—a cruel one—that he'd got exactly what he'd wanted when he'd been a kid—unsure and ashamed about feelings he couldn't control—and hated it. Like he couldn't win.

But at least he knew where they stood now. They both did. And maybe now they could actually move on, build something together. Ray hadn't wanted to be an omega, but he'd always wanted a family. He didn't regret that. And if Gabriel could see past his own shame and regret, he could be a lot more to the pack than an efficient leader.

It was harder with Josh. Josh had never left him. Ray had never had to accept that he could no longer rely on him. And Ray had never really managed to stop thinking about men in ways he knew weren't appropriate. And Josh had been there, so some of those thoughts had been about Josh. If one was that way inclined—and now Ray didn't need to pretend to himself about it anymore—then it was a little hard to ignore Josh's soft pink lips, hazel eyes and floppy blond hair combo. He remembered a particularly cold winter when they'd been thirteen when he had huddled into his coat all the way to and from school just so he could avoid looking at his best friend's reddened lips and flushed cheeks.

It'd felt like a betrayal to want something like that from Josh. He had always been so sure Josh would feel nothing but disgust if he knew, and not even because Ray was a boy, but because he was *Ray*. He was Josh's best friend and he wasn't meant to want something else.

It'd felt like a betrayal when Josh had done it too. When Josh had declared he wanted Ray. Just not the way Ray had always been. He wasn't that far in denial; if Josh had kissed him at thirteen, or fifteen, or the week before he'd presented...

But he hadn't. Only when Ray had become an omega, not just his friend but a desirable mate, had Josh declared his interest. Not in his best friend, but in the part of him that had been forced upon Ray by an accident of birth or circumstance. Josh had been the last person he had wanted to see him as an omega, and he had been the first there in the hall waiting to receive him, to...to take him.

He had more or less managed to stop thinking about running after they'd bred him, but the instinct that had made him flee his uncle's hall was still there, tugging at him. Half wild, half human, but all need. It didn't feel right, no matter how much he struggled. He couldn't stop what the wolf wanted—needed—and he couldn't stop his own thoughts and feelings, either. *Was it the same for Josh? Or was it just the wolf?*

He wanted to know. He just wasn't sure he was ready to ask.

"Ray?" Josh asked from behind him, and Ray turned around fast enough he stumbled. Josh didn't try to catch him. Of course not, Ray realised dumbly, it wouldn't really hurt *Ray* to fall to the ground. "Are you okay?"

For a moment, he didn't know the answer, then he blurted it out, "Do you like men?"

Josh blinked at him, smelling wary. And then he nodded. He didn't try to walk into the room, even though it was his own and, in all fairness, his wolf's territory.

"What about women? You always went with girls when we were kids."

Josh licked his lips nervously. "I like girls, too."

"So it's not just omegas..." Ray confirmed. "You would go for, I don't know, Alec."

Josh's face twisted. "I don't like *all* men, Ray. Definitely not Alec. But not just omegas," he added a little hesitantly.

He wanted to ask more, but he didn't think he could get through this if Josh said the wrong thing and, whatever he felt, they had to do this if he wanted to be safe during the full moon. He turned away from Josh, opening his jeans and kicking them off—they were loose since he had insisted on wearing them until he hadn't been able to close them anymore over his belly. Unlike Ray's abdomen, back to the usual flatness, no amount of washing would shrink them back. He sat heavily on the bed and glanced up at Josh, who hadn't moved. The door was still wide open beside him; anyone could have walked by and seen Ray half-naked. There wasn't anybody around who hadn't already seen it all, but his skin still itched.

"Are you coming?" he asked a little sharply.

Josh nodded and walked in, still looking confused. He could deal; Ray was confused as fuck and he could still do it, why should it be any different for Josh?

Josh pulled his shirt off, exposing the glowing skin of his chest. He dropped the shirt on the back of a chair and thumbed his jeans open with the lack of self-consciousness Ray had grown used to around shifters. The same confidence he'd lost himself. It hurt to remember, but even so, it was impossible not to watch.

Josh was beautiful; the planes of his chest culminating in pink nipples Ray wanted in his mouth, the dip of his hipbones calling to Ray's thumbs. He stepped closer, right up until his knees bumped Ray's. Ray looked up from the happy trail leading into his tented boxers to meet his face. Josh was already watching him, face soft and open. Ray pulled on his too long hair to get him to lean in close enough to take his mouth into a kiss. Once it started, Josh went for it full-tilt and soon he was on top of Ray, his legs bracketing Ray's thighs, his tongue exploring Ray's mouth, his hands holding onto Ray's biceps where the t-shirt he still wore left them exposed.

Ray arched into him, seeking contact. Josh gave it to him, grounding his hips down until their cocks were shoved together through two layers of cotton, each sliding against their own precome. Ray couldn't take it for long; he leaned back and hooked his left leg over Josh's hip to force him closer. That was all it took, he was getting wet for it. He groaned as Josh's arousal and need hit him and his body reacted, but he couldn't help squirming. He wanted Josh, he had wanted him before, but it was Josh's need that was affecting him so thoroughly now, like Ray's body was made to provide what an alpha needed of it.

"Oh, Ray," Josh moaned, grinding harder. "Please," he added incoherently, "Please, I want... I need to..."

Ray was regretting not taking off his underwear earlier, but he'd have felt stupid sitting there in just a t-shirt. Josh found his mouth again, feeding him his tongue like he would die if

Ray didn't suck on it. Ray didn't risk it; he tangled one of his hands into Josh's hair and smashed their lips together even as Josh's rhythm against his hip got more desperate and the wave of arousal inside him got more and more intense. The orgasm left him trembling as if his nerves were about to give out under the onslaught of sensations, both his and his alpha's.

It was only when Josh rolled off him and threw an arm around his middle to keep him close that he realised Josh hadn't actually done what he had gone there to do. Ray closed his eyes, too wiped out to be annoyed. He did like orgasms, after all, and this was certainly better than Gabriel's need for a repeat performance.

And then Josh's lips against his neck moved, tickling. It took Ray a moment to understand Josh was speaking, very quietly. If his lips hadn't been inches from Ray's ear, he probably wouldn't have heard.

"I like you," his friend said, and it sounded like an admission. It *had* to be an admission, following what Josh had said about liking men, even as Josh insisted, "I really like you, Ray."

Even as Ray arched into the soft, feathery kisses Josh was planting down his throat, he realised he wanted to know more. But the words wouldn't come. He let his eyes flutter closed to focus on the sensation of Josh's mouth and Josh's hand sliding up his naked thigh, pulling his shorts down. Whatever else Josh felt or didn't feel, *this* was true, he thought. His hands and his mouth and the way he was already hardening again against Ray's side. He hadn't asked about himself in particular, himself... before. He didn't know how.

He knew he was wanted, but he didn't know how to ask if he was loved.

He didn't know how to ask if it was him or the omega wolf. But that wasn't the real problem; he could have accepted either answer—painful as it might have been. It was something else that scared him: that maybe Josh couldn't tell the difference. And that... that Ray couldn't bear.

Josh didn't let him dwell on that for long; his hand encircled Ray's erection and Ray's hips pumped up of their own accord.

"God, you're gorgeous," Josh mumbled.

He leaned in and kissed Ray, soft and gentle until Ray opened his mouth and kissed him back, sloppy and wet and not careful at all. And Ray was wet again, still. Josh pushed him onto his back, bent his legs and climbed between them. It left his hole exposed and leaking. All he knew was Josh's mouth at his throat, and the utter emptiness he needed Josh to fill. His alpha didn't make him wait long, lodging himself in place and entering Ray with a well-placed thrust that had Ray involuntarily clenching hard. Josh froze on top of him, mouth wet with spit and eyes dilated in the darkening room. Ray saw the alarm on his face before he licked his lips and asked very quietly, like he wasn't half-buried in Ray's body, "Okay?"

In response, Ray got a leg behind his buttocks and pushed him forward and, as Josh sank into him fully, he wondered if there was a way to keep him there forever.

Josh hadn't knotted him, of course. If any of his alphas was capable of being careful during even the most passionate of sex, it was Josh.

If he hadn't been so relieved, Ray might have found it a little offensive. But that was stupid, he knew that. The sooner he got of any fantasies Iesu and Sergi might have got into his head about Josh being something other than one of his alphas, the better.

Chapter 5

Ray wasn't looking forward to the full moon, but he wasn't worried either. Maybe because the sex had gone well, or because Alec seemed fairly sure that he wouldn't conceive even if there was knotting, or simply because he was too busy to worry.

Josh had tried to volunteer to sit with the babies, but Gabriel had overruled him and declared it'd only be fair if it was a draw from a hat. Josh had opened his mouth to argue—probably with a sensible argument about how he loved babysitting—but Iesu had spoken up to give his support to Gabriel's proposal. That had thrown them all so much that they'd let Gabriel win. So now it was Iesu who was spending the night keeping five eager pups from wandering too far if their parents got too busy with each other.

"Are you sure his wolf will know it's on babysitting duty?" Ray asked Alec.

"Ray, it's always done this way," Gabriel reminded him. Ray knew it in theory, of course, but in his pack, he and other betas had been the ones in charge of his younger siblings and other kids during the full moon hunt. Of course, in his old pack, there had been so many betas, young and old, that they had been able to take turns easily, only missing a full moon every six months or so. "Iesu will stay with them the whole night. None of the wolves would walk off on them no matter what."

Back then, full moon duty had been something to complain about—pups also got excited—but the good ones had the potential to turn into a party of sorts. There were always plenty of snacks and fresh meat from the hunt, maybe a game of charades of a string of children's movies in the hall. Sometimes omegas who'd only recently given birth would join the betas in care duty, too, but that wasn't an option for Ray. Not with no other omegas in his new pack. Omegas might need alphas for sex, but alphas needed omegas to ground them.

If they ever got another omega, maybe Ray would be able to rest during a full moon, but as it was, he needed to participate in the run every month. It was hard work, but it wasn't safe to leave a bunch of alphas alone when their emotions were running high.

With an omega in their midst, they were guaranteed to choose sex over violence.

The night was clear, if a little cold, and the latter ceased to be a problem once they were in fur. To the wolf, the cold autumn night felt refreshing and full of possibility. The moon illuminating every one of the paths they might follow, reflecting on the pelt of any prey, and making the nearby lake separating them from Ray's birth pack shine silver.

He didn't wait for the alphas, just took off the moment he had paws—his wolf surging inside him like it'd been desperate for its freedom—and the world of smell and sound opened up to him like a new universe. He caught the trail of some rabbits and found himself following it, the plentiful dinner they'd shared already forgotten. The alphas showed up soon enough and it was simply enough to corner a couple of them until Alec could sink his teeth into a leg. Sergi managed a killing blow the first time around. He brought it to Ray as an offering. Ray's wolf didn't hesitate before tucking in—unlike his human side, it had no doubt that its mates were meant to provide for him.

He hadn't even licked his snout clean before he was off again, making the others choose between food and following. Gabriel had probably eaten already because he was on Ray's heels instantly, playfully trying to bite his tail and nudging his side with his bulkier form. Ray pushed on, overtaking him. He completely missed Josh coming from the other side until they were rolling together on the ground. He aimed a bite at his mate, making him pull back enough that he could roll away, and off they were again. But by then the others had caught up; Alec blocked his path and Josh threw himself at Ray again, tucking into him so their bodies and legs tangled and sent them both crashing. The omega wolf didn't think the game was over, but Sergi got his teeth around Ray's neck—just a tug, nowhere near pain—and Gabriel and Alec were blocking him from rolling. He went limp under Josh.

He could smell their interest; his own low-level arousal, banked during the hunt and the run, flamed up. He squirmed, suddenly needy. Alec howled, then the others joined in.

He shifted back and found he was hard and slick, hole already clenching. And before he had quite blinked the black and white out of his vision, his alphas were following. Josh was half covered in grass and his blond hair was a tangled mess, but he was smiling widely with pure joy. It was so easy for him to get in Ray; it wasn't until he was arching on his mate's cock that he caught sight of Gabriel and realised it was the first full moon his cousin hadn't demanded to go first. He didn't have long to think of it; his skin was on fire everywhere Josh touched him, and his insides felt like they'd explode, the need so intense he could hardly let Josh fuck into him without squirming away. He clenched his eyes shut as Josh finally orgasmed, sweeping him into his pleasure like he was yanking him along onto a rollercoaster ride.

He became conscious of his surroundings again as Josh leaned forward and kissed him deeply before withdrawing his hips, come spilling out of Ray's body and onto the grass between his legs. He closed his eyes for a moment at the discomfort and the next thing he knew, Gabriel was on top of him, lifting his knees and lodging himself into his body like fitting a missing piece. He watched Ray's face as he rolled his hips, so intense it made Ray look away. But this time, Gabriel didn't allow it. He leaned closer and put a hand on Ray's face, forcing him to look up at him. Ray shivered violently in his grasp, overwhelmed by the intimacy of it as his sensitive body was brought to hardness again, but as close as they were, he couldn't miss Gabriel's expression. He was desperate to come, like any man in the middle of fucking, but he was also... concentrating. On Ray.

Ray scrunched his eyes shut; he couldn't... It was too much. And maybe Gabriel was paying close enough attention to see it because right then he sped up into sharp, short thrusts, nails digging into Ray's hips to keep him in the right position as he pistoned in and out of him. Ray threw his head back, desperate to come as Gabriel got closer. Too much was happening around him at once: the scents of blood and sweat, his mates surrounding him, and the feeling of his body about to break... Gabriel let out a pained sound and leaned forward to suck on the mark he had left on Ray's neck as he emptied himself into Ray's clenching arsehole. And Ray was coming too, his cock spilling again, adding to the mess all over his front as Gabriel's pleasure washed over him in waves.

A second orgasm in such quick succession was too much for his brain to handle and he lost some time. Gabriel was out of his body when he blinked his eyes open. He stared at his mate, realising what it meant: Gabriel hadn't knotted him, he had... His lips parted, maybe to thank him, but Gabriel moved aside before he could gather his thoughts. Alec took his place.

Ray let himself be rolled onto his front and got on his hands and knees, just like his mate preferred. Alec was smaller and he could penetrate Ray deeper this way. He entered easily, as could be expected by the seed of two alphas and Ray's own slick still dripping down his buttocks. Alec moved in deep and fast, again and again. He didn't try to touch Ray's cock, knowing he was too sensitive for direct contact after coming twice, and Ray could relax into it. And then Alec froze into one of his strokes, buried fully inside him. Ray tensed under him. Alec *wouldn't*... He heard the slap to Alec's side before he could quite process it reverberating through their joined bodies. There were no words and he wasn't sure who it had been, but it got Alec moving again and soon enough brought the release of orgasm. It almost hurt, but the relief would have been worth a lot more than pain.

Sergi hadn't been able to wait for any repositioning, simply taking Alec's place and shoving into Ray, rutting hard and fast into his exhausted body. It did hurt, but he didn't care. He just wanted the first round to be over so he could be sure none of them would lose it and knot him. Sergi tugged too roughly on his hips to keep himself buried deep as he discharged, hot come trapped in Ray's passage by his unrelenting thrusts. And Ray was just grateful for the support staying upright—his knees felt like they'd give at any moment and his arms weren't much better. His own dick trembled weakly, leaking desultorily down his thigh.

He let himself close his eyes after that, and they did what they needed to do: taking turns using him as he lay on the ground. By the time the moon gave way to the sun and Gabriel picked him up, none of them had knotted him.

They helped him shower and tucked him into bed with the pups around him.

He couldn't ask for more.

Chapter 6

"**A**re you...?" Ray's throat closed up, heart battering against his chest. He looked between Josh and Iesu. "Are you serious?"

"Yes," Iesu said gently. Josh was just standing there, smiling gently.

"Are you *sure*?" Ray insisted, leaning back against the kitchen counter. He felt he might lose his balance at any moment.

Josh came out of his daze and stepped closer, taking Ray's face into his hands and meeting his eyes. "Yes," he promised, low and certain. "He said yes. We can have five betas. Your sister has volunteered and Iesu went around talking to other young betas, so we'll have a list a mile long by the end of the week."

Ray exhaled, nothing close enough to a laugh. He closed his eyes, but at least he wasn't crying. He blinked and tilted his head back, dizzy with relief, and then Josh was enveloping him in his arms, bringing him forward against the strength of his body. And it wasn't just his body; he had come through for Ray, he had come through for *the pack*.

After a few minutes, Iesu cleared his throat and Ray looked up and pushed Josh back a little, feeling his face heat up. "Sorry," he told Iesu, "I haven't even thanked you."

Iesu shook his head with an easy smile before Ray could try and hug him too. "No need, I..." He licked his lips, shifting in place. "I do have some bad news."

Ray paused, then nodded for him to go ahead.

"You have to tell Nicholas and the others that they have to go."

"Oh," Ray said, feeling like all the air had been punched out of his lungs, "I... I said I would take them in."

"Yes," Iesu agreed, "and now you're taking it back. Because you can afford to, and Nicholas will be annoyed, but he'll accept it. It'd have been... a lot for you. He can't think you want that, not really."

Ray's eyes met Josh's and his friend nodded, reaching to take Ray's hand in his own. "You have to, Ray. It's not just for you, it's what's best for the pack too."

And Ray couldn't argue with that, so he nodded, even if the idea of breaking his word set his stomach churning.

The house didn't have any spare rooms, so Nicholas and his friends had been sleeping in their tents, but Ray had made sure they were invited in for meals. They'd gone past Ray's borders and camped out in those same tents during the last full moon. It was simply too dangerous to have wolves who didn't belong when emotions were running high. But they'd been back for a week now.

They had been talking about building a second house instead of expanding the first since it made sense for Ray to live with his mates and for the new alphas to have their own space to invite their own mates to live with them eventually.

It'd been as good as done.

And now he was just going to say no to all that, to Nicholas's plans of changing the fence and getting a decent timing belt for Josh's Jeep, to his kindness and understanding. And he was sorry for it, sorry he was taking back something he had given already, in word if not in deed. But he didn't regret it; he didn't want it. The idea that he wouldn't have to balance having sex with eleven alphas in a single night was enough to make him sit down and shake with relief, without even going into the matter of pregnancy.

Nicholas had come inside gladly like he had any time Ray had wanted him in the past.

"What's up?" he asked, smiling at Ray shyly—he could never quite hide his pleasure at Ray's presence, at Ray's *promise*.

"Please take a seat," Ray asked, and he knew Nicholas hadn't missed the stiffness in his voice. His expression had gone serious and worried. But he sat and waited. He had been waiting for almost a month already, and he'd agreed to wait even longer to get what he wanted just because Ray had made him a promise.

Ray took his own seat at the edge of the opposite sofa and glanced at his hands in his lap, trying to summon the words to his lips. "I have some bad news."

"Okay," the alpha said when Ray didn't continue.

Ray made himself meet his eyes. He owed him that much, at least. "My uncle has agreed some of his betas can join my pack."

"*Your* pack?" Nicholas repeated, voice even but tense.

"I'm sorry," Ray said. "I know I said I would—"

"You more than said you would," Nicholas interrupted. "You promised. You…"

"I know!" Ray said. Taking back his word was making him sick already; if it hadn't been for Josh's reminder that he was doing it for the pack… "And I'm sorry, but it was my only choice and it was… it was terrible. I'm only one man, I can't—"

"Do you think you would be the first omega to have a lot of alphas?" Nicholas asked. "How do you think the great packs survived?"

"I don't *want* it," Ray snapped, angry. Nicholas wasn't his alpha; he had a right to be disappointed, but he couldn't make any demands of Ray.

Nicholas's angry expression seemed to shatter. He looked off to the side, stiff as a board, and slowly exhaled. "You are right, I'm… I'm out of line. It is your decision."

"I'm sorry I'm breaking my promise," Ray added. "I do feel bad about it."

Nicholas didn't look at him; just sat there like he was barely keeping himself from shouting again. Ray didn't need to hear his heart skip a beat to know he was lying, the sudden controlled calm in his voice gave it away. "It's quite alright, it's… it's perfectly natural that you'd be scared of having so many alphas to please."

"Thank you for understanding," Ray replied, ignoring the jibe at his courage. It *was* perfectly normal to be afraid, whatever it sounded like when Nicholas said it like that. And Nicholas was being moderately graceful about the whole thing, even if they both knew he didn't really understand.

"We'll be out of your territory by nightfall," Nicholas announced, getting to his feet and still not looking at Ray.

"Don't worry about it, tomorrow's fine too," Ray offered even though, in truth, he'd have much rather have them gone. The sooner he didn't have to see Nicholas, the sooner he could forget his own mistake.

He'd have thought that was enough awkwardness to last him for a while, but it'd been a week since the first full moon in which he had slept with his alphas. The change in atmosphere had been noticeable. It was like a dam had broken: they were all touching him more, aware of his presence in a way they hadn't been for a while, or at least had successfully hidden from Ray.

Gabriel caught him in the kitchen and plastered himself against Ray's back as he made some tea. He was close enough that Ray could tell he wasn't hard, but he smelt warmth and welcoming like he... like he wanted Ray. He nuzzled at Ray's neck, stubble rasping against the sensitive skin. Ray froze with his hand in the kettle. Did Gabriel expect him to...?

"Can I have a cuppa?" came the whispered request. Ray startled a little but nodded. His cousin stepped back to let him reach for a second cup.

He concentrated on getting rid of the teabag—Gabriel liked his tea weak—and adding milk to his own drink before turning around to face his alpha. Gabriel was already watching him. Their eyes met. "You're still nervous," he said.

Ray put his cup on the kitchen table and, to his surprise, Gabriel took a seat. Ray didn't, just leaned back against the counter a couple steps away. But he needed those steps, just a little space to know he could move away if he wanted to. He picked up the cup again and took a sip, letting the flavour and warmth fill him up. "Yeah," he said.

"Fair enough," Gabriel said softly. He was staring into his cup like he could read his future in its depths. "Am I doing something to make you nervous?"

"Well, you..." Ray trailed off, unsure. It wasn't that Gabriel had done anything wrong today. He'd come into the kitchen and hugged Ray, not mentioning the fact that he very much wanted Ray to go to bed with him despite it being obvious to them both. "Not really. Not now."

That made Gabriel stiffen, but Ray didn't think he was surprised. He hoped he wasn't angry, either, but it was hard to tell without seeing his face. His heartbeat only told Ray that he was mildly agitated.

"I can go," he gritted out finally. He couldn't manage anything close to neutral and he still wasn't looking at Ray. But for the first time, Ray realised the anger wasn't directed at him.

"No."

Gabriel glanced up, frowning but hopeful.

Ray licked his lips. "You remember what we talked about?"

"Of course." Ray waited, sipping at his drink but not looking away, until Gabriel finally seemed to get that wasn't enough. "Ask you, and foreplay?" he offered, oddly tentative.

Ray nodded, essaying a smile that didn't feel quite natural. But hey, they were both trying.

Gabriel exhaled, then tried his own smile. "Can I kiss you?"

Ray nodded, watching him get to his feet, shirt pulling on his shoulders as he moved, eyes intent on Ray. Only when his cousin gently took it from his hands, did he notice he was still holding the cup. Gabriel leaned closer and put his lips against Ray's cheek. Ray shivered, then turned his head till their lips met in a soft whisper. Gabriel's breath hitched and his hands found purchase on Ray's waist. Ray didn't think he meant to, but one of his fingers slid under the fabric and onto Ray's bare skin, sending a shot of wanting through him. And then they were kissing, tongues tangling and teeth nipping.

Ray found himself growing pliant in his cousin's arms, but Gabriel pulled back and found his eyes. "Don't fall asleep," he whispered, pulling him from the daze of lust he'd got used to falling into. He tried kissing Gabriel back, he liked the feeling of his stubble against his own bare cheeks and the smoothness of his teeth against his own tongue. He smelt good too: masculine, and a little sweaty, and *Ray's*.

It was still Gabriel who had to stop them and suggest they move to the bedroom. But it was a suggestion, even if refusing at that stage seemed beyond ridiculous to Ray. Ray let Gabriel lead him to the bed and pull his shirt off before laying him down on his back—but he did have enough willpower to drag his cousin on top of him. Gabriel opened their trousers and took their cocks out. "Is this good?"

Ray didn't see how the angle could work; and then the heavy, hot weight of Gabriel's cock pressed against his own and his cousin pulled on them both. Ray thrust hard enough that if Gabriel had been any lighter, he might have thrown him off the bed. As it was, it made their wet cocks slide together and both of them moan. They came like that, kissing so clumsily it was closer to panting in each other's faces. Afterwards, Gabriel turned enough to rest his face in the curve of Ray's neck, shifting his hips to the side to give their oversensitive cocks a break.

His teeth were right next to Ray's neck, but it was still such a vulnerable position to arrange himself into that it made him want to say something. There wasn't much more to say, though, so he put his arm around Gabriel instead and held him close.

The others took their cue from that. Iesu had been twitchy as hell since the full moon. He'd stayed with the pups all night long just like he'd promised, but that meant he hadn't been with Ray at all. Ray wasn't surprised that night when he asked if Ray wanted to come look at some furniture on his computer after dinner. Ray had known the blowjob he'd provided the morning after the full moon couldn't be enough to satisfy the alpha, but he'd been too sore for more fucking, and Iesu too much of a gentleman to say anything. He wondered if Sergi was making up for the difference, but somehow it felt wrong to ask them about their relationship. They'd chosen each other and they chose what to do together.

And they always seemed to choose to *be* together, so Ray wasn't surprised to find Sergi, shirtless and sleepy, on Iesu's bed. His alpha lifted his head and twisted to the side to blink at him, eyes bright and pleased. Ray thought about painting him like that: the muscles of his back in stark contrast with the red coverlet, the curve of his arse painted on his tight jeans. He approached the bed without speaking and swung a leg over one of Sergi's half spread ones. The alpha raised himself on his elbows and twisted to look at him curiously, his eyes dark and cheeks flushed with sleep and something more. Ray remembered his face flushing in anger, his body tense under Ray's when they fought... He couldn't believe he'd tricked himself into thinking it was all about wiping the smug look off his rival's face.

He'd wanted this: Sergi under him, making no objections to Ray's superior position, going down easily with a pleased rumble when Ray put his hands on his lower back and slid them up towards his neck. It had never been just been about winning...

"Wow," Iesu said from the doorway, towel slung low on his hips and watching them with evident delight. "I should be late more often."

Ray shrugged and Sergi made a noise he couldn't quite parse, but Iesu actually glanced at his desk where Ray saw his laptop was open and still on. "I really wanted to show you the shelving..." he lamented. From under Ray's massaging hands, Sergi snorted his disbelief.

Iesu laughed, mostly at himself. "Okay, okay, you're right," he agreed and dropped the towel, exposing his beautifully tanned skin. He had to have spent the summer swimming naked in the lake because there was no interruption to the smooth honeyed colour of his skin. He had a few curls around his nipples and leading down the centre of his chest and abdomen, where there was proof of how much he liked the view. His cock was red and hard and shiny with precome.

Ray only realised that he was staring when Sergi shifted under him too abruptly and he had to lean forward to keep his balance, accidentally pressing his own erection against Sergi's arse. Sergi groaned and before he knew it, Ray found himself being pushed down into the bedding, Sergi slotting his own leg between Ray's and pressing his knee against his cock. Ray whimpered, struggling against Sergi's hold on his wrists. He didn't really want to get away; he needed more as much as he needed less. Sergi gave it to him, leaning in and taking his mouth in a brutal kiss, wet and hard, accompanied by the thrust of Sergi's jean-clad erection onto Ray's stomach and the pressure of his leg against Ray's crotch. His shirt had ridden up and he was desperately conscious that it was barely covering the upper part of his chest. He could feel each thrust in his nipples, erect and still sensitive over flesh not quite as firm as it had been a year earlier.

Iesu joined them on the bed, crawling on Ray's other side and sneaking a hand between them to open first Ray's, then Sergi's zipper. Sergi allowed it, but he didn't seem ready to get off Ray long enough to get naked. Not until Iesu kissed his cheek and teasingly brought his mouth to his own, taking Sergi's passionate kisses for himself and allowing Ray to get a breath under them both.

"Off," he said, pulling at his lover's trousers when they parted.

Sergi grumbled but obediently rolled to the side to shuck it all off. Iesu took the chance to pull on Ray's cuffs. Ray obligingly raised his hips for it and soon he was in just his shirt, hard and exposed, and Iesu had hold of him. He went easily when Iesu rolled him to lean back on Sergi, now fully naked, and then knelt between Ray's legs himself.

"If we could only both go at once." He sighed, more at Sergi than at Ray.

Sergi twitched under Ray, obviously liking the image. The movement slid his cock into the leaking space between Ray's buttocks, making him squirm. He was ready for penetration, of course, just like any omega would be when an alpha wanted him. Iesu's eyes gleamed when he added, looking directly at Ray, "Do you think you could take it?"

Ray trembled, whether at the surge of lust or fear, he couldn't say. But it was apparently too much for Sergi because his hands were clamping around Ray's hip and middle to lift him up. He sat back against the headboard and drew Ray to him. Iesu took hold of Ray's upper arms and helped him kneel so that Sergi's cock could be introduced into his body. Ray let himself be pulled back down to take the whole length into his body, shuddering at the fullness of it as they made him sit on Sergi's lap. He had never been penetrated from below before, he realised. He didn't have long to think though, because as Sergi started moving, Iesu brought Ray closer and started kissing him. It was not his usual soft and tender kisses either; he licked into Ray's mouth as if he had to take every moan his lover was dragging from Ray's throat or die. Ray clutched at him, too gone on the pleasure of Sergi's cock deep within him and Sergi's and Iesu's own need to do more than hold on.

Iesu crawled closer and knelt between Ray's thighs, pressing his naked thigh deliciously against Ray's dick for a moment and pushing him down even more fully onto Sergi's engorged cock. His own erection left a line of heat as it dragged against Ray's left thigh, but he shifted away almost at once. He lifted Ray's knees, bending him double against Sergi's chest. Ray squirmed where he was impaled. He felt Iesu's fingers brushing his now exposed arsehole and Sergi's cock going into it. Sergi groaned as Ray was moved on him, and Ray let his head fall back on his shoulder, whimpering at the combination of the light touch of Iesu's fingers and the overwhelming fullness of Sergi fucking him.

Was Iesu really going to put it in him too? He couldn't find the words to ask, or to protest. Iesu nudged his own leg between Sergi's and then his cock was pushing into the space between Ray's arse cheeks, slick with his own juices and Sergi's precome. Ray whined low in his throat. He was going to do it, he realised. They were truly going to share him. He wondered if they would stop if they really hurt him, or if their own pleasure would make it feel good to him when their cocks met inside his body. Would it still feel good if they made him bleed? How far did the alpha magic really go?

Iesu lowered his hands to Ray's buttocks and pressed them together, holding his dick tight between them, then he started to thrust. Ray convulsed, the sensation of Iesu's cock sliding against his balls as Sergi surged into his arse was almost too much to bear without coming. And then his brain processed that it wasn't happening. Iesu hadn't been serious. His alpha sped up his pace, slicking up Ray's buttocks and thighs with his arousal. Sergi's big cock in him felt like a relief compared to what he'd been expecting, and then they shifted his hips and the head of Sergi's dick pushed directly against his prostate, lighting him up. Ray squirmed, begging for release without words and pushing back for more. But he couldn't come. He needed...

Fortunately, Sergi only managed a couple of aborted thrusts into him before he was clutching at Ray's arms too, fingers interlacing with Iesu's, and coming hard, teeth sinking into the back of Ray's shoulder. Iesu sped up, groaning, and took hold of Ray's neck to leave his own mark. Sergi's orgasm was still coursing through Ray's body when Iesu's began. The alphas held him as he convulsed with pleasure, sobbing with relief as the tension finally broke. He thought he had lost consciousness for a moment because when he blinked his eyes open again he could feel his cheeks were wet with tears.

They laid him down on the bed between them, and Iesu even managed to get a blanket to cover them all before they fell asleep.

And then there was Josh. It shouldn't have been so different; he had had sex with Josh before his heat. Hell, he had asked him if he was attracted to men and Josh had clearly understood that it was a personal question. But it was like now that he had begun, he couldn't stop thinking about all the other things he wanted to ask.

None of the reasons he had given Iesu and Sergi had changed. He and Josh were bound for life, whatever happened between them would never go away. Without the possibility of stopping, the idea of beginning was beyond terrifying... And he was First Omega of his pack, they had to come first. Maybe he couldn't stop himself from feeling, especially not when he had pretty much admitted to it. He certainly couldn't avoid Josh and the more of Josh he saw, the more he wanted to see.

The more he wanted to have.

To say he wasn't in the mood to go to bed with his friend would have been an understatement of epic proportions. He wanted Josh, naturally—and not simply because Josh wanted him—but he also knew that every moment spent together was a moment he risked giving himself away.

Josh wouldn't have asked for it if he hadn't needed it, though. It wasn't a matter of pleasure only; alphas needed to have sex with their omegas regularly to feel secure in their bond. He would have suffered if Ray had asked him for a break, but he would have wanted to know if there was something wrong. And Ray couldn't explain why it was him specifically that he didn't want to be intimate with... It just wouldn't work.

He opened his door in just his underwear and invited Josh in. He kissed him by the door with as much honest interest as he could summon when he wanted to throw himself on the bed and hide his face instead. Josh noticed he was a little stiff and pulled back and checked his expression. Whatever he thought he saw on Ray's face slowed him down, but it didn't make him stop. Of course, it only made it harder to have him planting soft, tiny kisses along Ray's neck and ear—more teasing than sensual—and Ray struggled not to squirm, wanting things fast and passionate. He needed Josh's overwhelming desire to cover up for his own very mixed feelings: he wanted Josh, but he also wanted to *know*. He wanted to ask so badly, he was starting to think the answer—any answer—might provide more relief than an orgasm.

He whimpered when Josh dragged a hand down his stomach and into his underwear, circling his cock loosely before sliding the tips of his fingers through the wetness between Ray's legs. The sensitive nerves of his arsehole seemed directly connected to his cock and when his mate pushed his fingers inside, he arched into it, suddenly desperate. Josh had to take his fingers out so he could drag Ray to the bed. He only paused to push Ray's underwear down his legs and help him step out of it. And then they were on top of the covers and Ray barely had time to get his knees up before his friend finally pressed his hips forwards and fitted his cock inside. The relief was enough to distract him from the pain of the sudden stretch. Josh paused for a moment before hitching his hips up to force Ray to take his entire length. Ray groaned, overwhelmed, and wriggled, trying to adjust to the hot weight inside of him.

He should have been used to it, as many times as he had been fucked. But, slick and all, it was still always a struggle to accept another body into his own. Josh knew what he bear, of course, and when he started moving into him, it was no more than Ray could take—intense but not painful. He turned his head for it when his alpha leaned in closer and captured his mouth and even though he was struggling for air, he kissed back. It felt like he could never stop kissing back, like was pouring himself down into that kiss and when he was all gone, he would die from it.

Josh pulled away. His eyes were wild and he was gasping, flushed and feverish. Ray looked right back at him for a moment. It felt like staring into the sun. "Ray..." Josh whispered, and then again, "*Ray*."

Ray didn't glance back up. Josh was fully seated inside him, Ray's legs bracketing his hips, as close as another person could get. Ray clenched around him, pushing up into it, and Josh's hips stuttered in an aborted thrust. He grunted with the effort of keeping still. "Ray, what..."

Ray shook his head, still not meeting his eyes again. If he did, he thought he'd shatter into a million pieces. And then Josh seemed to understand what he needed because he started moving faster, in and out, faster and harder. Ray let his eyes flutter closed and he leaned back on the pillows. He relaxed when he felt Josh's mouth sucking a bruise on the skin of his neck on top of the mark his teeth had left on Ray's skin forever.

It lasted for a long time; Ray's cock was hard but the arousal came and went, peaking before receding again, a capricious ocean mocking him. Ray risked opening his eyes to check on Josh and his friend groaned as their eyes met. And just like that, he was coming. Ray felt the warmth of it deep inside even as he clenched and arched as his own orgasm rushed through him, like a flood that left nothing standing.

Josh pulled out of him too fast and half collapsed on his side, their warm, sweaty skin sticking together. It was still too hot, but Ray needed to breathe more than he needed to cool down, so he stayed still, both of them panting with the effort of getting enough air.

"Ray?" Josh asked after a minute.

"Mmm?"

"Ray?" Josh was leaning on his elbow, looking down at him. He was still flushed, but his concern was plain to see on his face. "Please tell me if I did anything wrong."

Ray froze, glancing up at him. He hadn't used any type of compulsion, but it was still Ray's alpha asking and his wolf wanted to give whatever was asked. "You didn't," he said, keeping it short.

Josh opened his mouth, but then seemed to think better of it and closed it again. He still looked worried. "But you will tell me if I ever do."

"Sure," Ray said. And it turned out he could lie, at least about something as vague as his intentions.

"Okay," Josh said. He was still half-draped around Ray. He seemed to be waiting for something, but Ray didn't know what, and apparently neither did Josh because he just said it again and got up. "I promised to help with the dishes."

Ray buried his face in the sheets, groaning in frustration when the scent of their bodies hit him. He turned his face and tried to breathe through his mouth. He wasn't an idiot; he'd hurt Josh. Or at the very least offended him, and things were still fragile enough between them that Josh hadn't dared to push it further.

Josh hadn't become his alpha to have power over him, Ray knew this like he knew the sun rose in the mornings and the moon ruled his existence. But it was a consequence neither of them could control nor change. Josh could no longer be the pushy best friend with Ray's best interest at heart behind his hearty teasing. He was responsible for Ray in a way nobody had been since he'd been a child, and he knew it too well. He was afraid of it. Maybe more than Ray was himself. He asked Ray too often what he wanted when he'd been confident to assume before, and it hurt. But it didn't matter how much Ray wanted Josh to treat him like nothing had changed; the only way Josh could know that he wasn't abusing his alpha power with Ray was to ask him. Ray couldn't even say he didn't agree; he'd asked Gabriel exactly for that. It was what he *needed*. Not as an omega, as a person. To *feel* like a person. It was just that it was impossible to be with Josh and not miss the person he used to be, the freedom he used to have.

But it wasn't all about Ray, either. His alphas needed things, too, and not just sex. Ray hated being an omega, but suddenly he understood he'd have hated being an alpha too. He was already fucking terrified of messing up his kids' lives; he couldn't even fathom having that kind of control over an adult who could and should make their own choices.

But Josh knew. And Ray hadn't spared a single thought for how he might feel about it, even as Josh had bent over backwards to accommodate Ray's omega status.

It was what an alpha was meant to do, but it that didn't make it right.

Ray wasn't any less capable than they were of making an effort; he'd just been in too much pain and too worried about the babies to take the time.

But whether he was in love with Josh, whether he'd been for years, he was certain of one thing: Josh was the best friend he'd ever had. He deserved better than rushing to fulfil every single of Ray's needs while his own were ignored.

Ray would give them both a little space and then... Then he'd man up and be honest.

He just needed a little time to find the words. And the courage.

Alec had borrowed some equipment from the surgery where he'd started working part-time so he could do a full check-up of the babies at home.

"Do you really need to record everything every two weeks?" Ray asked, passing Clara over. When Alec had started with the check-ups early on, Ray had been happy that he was being thorough. Werewolves didn't really get sick, but Ray was a first-time father and he wasn't any less susceptible to that special brand of paranoia than a garden variety human.

"For their health? Not so much, no, but how are we ever going to figure out what's normal for werewolf babies if we don't have a baseline?"

Ray gave him a look and asked, "You are using our kids for science?" It came out more serious than he intended but before he could clarify or take it back, Alec was already rolling his eyes at him.

"I hardly think statistics count as being used as guinea pigs, Ray."

He was right, of course, but Ray was more intrigued by his confidence. He was still pretty shy around Ray, but bring up anything relating to biology and he turned into a total know-it-all. It was a startling contrast. "Did you get a really good grade on your degree or something? You always think you know everything."

Alec shrugged, writing down Clara's height on the laptop he'd balanced safely out of reach on top of the microwave. "I got a first. But it's not that I think much of myself, these are basic concepts."

Ray was silent for a long moment. He'd done biology up to GSCEs, it wasn't like he didn't know the basics. And he had decided to do art and design in college, he was hardly going to learn about human or wolf biology even if he hadn't had had to leave…

"Ray?"

He looked up, then took Clara into his arms and held her close. Her scent relaxed something in him and after a moment he put her down and called Michael, who had to be talked into abandoning fur in favour of skin with a lot of behind the ears rubbing. Alec took the squirming baby boy in silence—Ray could feel him holding back.

"I was thinking of college." He made himself say it. He had to stop hiding. Alec was his mate and he wanted to make Ray happy, but how could he be expected to succeed when Ray wouldn't tell him what happiness looked like for him? "I mean, I was just kidding about the science."

"Oh, okay," Alec said.

"It just made me think of school… I never really liked it, but college seemed nice." He shrugged. "I wasn't sure about design, but the art bits were… cool."

"You could go back," Alec offered. Ray glanced around the room, which was a mess after having the five babies crawling around for less than an hour. Alec reached over and took hold of Ray's wrist, gripping until Ray looked up. "You can. We have betas now, remember? And anyway, it's just a mess, it's not going to hurt anybody."

For a moment, Ray felt the hope surge in his chest. And just as swiftly reality crushed it. "How am I going to explain being pregnant?"

Alec's grip slackened. "Well... There's... Some people who are men can get pregnant. It happens."

Ray snorted. "Here? Where do you think we are? London? New York? They'd..." He stopped, swallowing. "Let's finish this," he asked, trying to keep his voice even.

Alec's hand hesitated on his arm, and then, almost too fast, he picked Mikey up from the scale he'd borrowed and shoved him into Ray's arms. Ray scrambled to close his arms around him. "What...?"

He glared at Alec, who looked pained. "Sorry, I just... I know you don't want me to hug you."

"What?" Ray asked, mystified, even as Mikey snuffled into his neck.

Alec looked down. "I know you don't like me, Ray, you don't have to pretend. You try your best and I appreciate it, but—"

"Wait, stop," Ray interrupted, and had to push his wolf down when it tried to make him quieten down. "That's not true. I... I hardly *know* you, Alec."

"You hardly know Iesu, and Sergi," Alec pointed out, "and you used to hate him, but now..."

"We are just..." Ray paused, at a loss for words. "You and me, we are very different people. You're a doctor, for god's sake, and I didn't even go to college for a month."

"What does it matter?" Alec asked, and he seemed genuinely confused. "Why do you need to go anywhere to be someone worth knowing?"

"Do you like *me*?" Ray asked incredulously. He knew Alec was attracted to him and cared for him as far as a mate would, but he'd never thought that had anything to do with who Ray was instead of *what* he was.

"Yes, Ray," Alec said sadly. "How can you not know that? I think you are beautiful and smart and brave." His eyes were stuck to the scale between them, but he didn't stop talking, like this was a truth as unquestionable as any scientific fact. "You practically raised your siblings even though you were only a kid yourself and when you presented omega, you put your chin up and you just went ahead. I can't even imagine how hard it's been for you and you never... You never give up. You take a little time to lick your wounds and then you're up again swinging like it's *nothing*. Of course I like you! And I could—"

"I'm sorry," Ray said softly, rubbing Mikey's back before putting him down on the floor so he could crawl away. He stared at Alec for a moment longer. "I do, you know."

"What?"

"I want a hug from you, and I care about you. And I like it when you're sure of yourself. You shouldn't put yourself down so much, it makes... it makes me angry, really, that you would do that when you have accomplished so much."

Alec's frown cleared, but he still glanced at their feet to make sure the ground was clear before he pulled Ray into an embrace. Ray held him back, clawing at his back to pull him closer.

"Stop hiding," he bit out, low and serious, and he might have been speaking to Alec.

Chapter 7

Taking your own advice was hard work. He'd been putting off talking to Josh for long enough—it'd been two days since his conversation with Alec... And more than a week since he'd slept with Josh. His friend wasn't exactly avoiding him, but in a house full of children, there was always something that needed doing and Josh liked doing it. Except that he normally took the time to sit with Ray and the others and watch TV, and now he acted like any time Ray sat down, he was needed to cover whatever Ray had stopped doing. He answered normally if Ray spoke to him and he offered him help even more often than he usually did, but he didn't linger.

Ray hadn't even noticed how often his friend would lean against a doorway or the side of a sofa and just chat, rocking a baby to sleep as he whispered with Ray about their old pack, or TV, or the laundry.

But it was impossible not to miss him now that he'd stopped.

It was even worse because Ray knew that all he had to do was ask and Josh would sit with him again. He probably wouldn't have asked for an explanation of the weird vibe between them—just assumed it was Ray freaking out about being an omega again.

Sometimes Ray thought Josh was too good to be true, other times he thought he was trying too hard not to get in Ray's way—like he felt he owed Ray for being his alpha and planned to be paying him back for the rest of their lives.

It wasn't like that. Neither of them had chosen to present as they had. And maybe Josh had chosen to mate Ray first, but he'd also offered Ray an out—unappetizing as it had been—and Ray hadn't taken it. Ray had been angry before, but he was done with it now; he had to be. Josh wasn't perfect—and neither were the other alphas—but they were *trying*. Ray really believed that; they were all trying their best to be good to him in as much as their biology allowed them to. They just didn't understand what it was like.

Except maybe Josh did, maybe he felt as odd being an alpha as Ray felt being an omega, as lost in his own body and its strange needs as Ray did. It wasn't the same, but Ray would take any true sympathy in a heartbeat.

It was all he could really accept from Josh, even if... But there was no point thinking about ifs and could-haves. It was what it was.

"Josh?" he said as soon as he walked into the living room. His friend looked up. Iesu and Sergi also perked up from their slumps in front of the TV and glanced his way before very pointedly turning their attention back to their own damn businesses.

"Yeah?"

"Can you help me with something?" Ray asked.

There was no reason to lie, or even try for discretion, but suddenly he couldn't stand the idea of giving even a hint of what was going on to the others.

Josh rolled Sasha onto her side so she was curled around Sergi's leg instead of his own and got to his feet.

By the time they walked into his bedroom, Ray's heartbeat was too fast to disguise.

"What's wrong?" Josh asked as the door closed with a click behind them.

Ray clenched his fists and made himself turn to face him. "Nothing. I mean, I have something to say, but you don't have to worry. It's not... everything's okay. Really."

Josh didn't look convinced, but he nodded. "What do you need help with?"

"Nothing," Ray said. "I mean, I just want to talk to you."

"But you didn't want them to know?" Josh guessed.

Ray ignored the question, instead, he exhaled once and then spoke as slowly as he could make himself. "I'm sorry I made things weird." He kept his eyes firmly on Josh's left shoulder. "I've been—"

"Don't be sorry," Josh jumped to reassure him. "I know how hard it's been..."

Ray raised a hand to stop him. "Just let me talk," he asked, then, realising how sharp he sounded, added, "please."

Josh nodded, eyes wide and alarmed, and leaned back against the door, like he needed the support. No, Ray realised, like *he wanted to look smaller than Ray.*

It was stupid, but it did help. His wolf was calm with his mate, even if it was confused by Ray's discomfort and the distance between them—wolves were social creatures, tactile and affectionate with mates and pups. Ray lowered his gaze all on his own.

"I have... feelings for you," he managed to say. Josh's breathing hitched, but Ray didn't look up to see what his expression revealed and he stayed quiet just like Ray had asked. "For a while now, I guess. From before." He licked his lips, feeling his face flaming. "I guess I should have guessed I would be an omega when you presented alpha. But even before—"

"No," Josh bit out. And Ray looked up; it sounded like the word had been ripped from him and he looked like he was struggling to stop there. When Ray didn't speak again, he continued, "I... Sorry, but you can't think that. This is *not* an instinct, it's not the mating drive or anything—Anything but us. Whatever it is, it's between us. It has always been there."

"How can you even tell?" Ray whispered back, hope surging in his chest against all reason and sense.

Josh stayed where he was, but his body tensed like it was an effort. "Because I have loved you for as long as I can remember. But I have been in love with you for at least five years." He said the words like it cost him nothing, like he had just been waiting for Ray to tell him it was okay to speak them.

Ray gaped at him, mind racing to do the math. They'd been thirteen back then. He glanced up at this friend. "Before I was an omega."

"And before I was an alpha," Josh confirmed.

"But it could still be—I don't know; we were already teenagers."

"Ray," Josh said, voice thin. "I... I'm not going to tell you how you feel, okay? If you think..." He exhaled and straightened even as he lowered his gaze like he couldn't bear to look at Ray. "I will believe you, whatever you tell me is true for you, I will believe you. But I won't let you take this away from me."

Ray froze, staring at him. Of course, Josh had assumed this meant things would change between them. "Take what? We are not—"

Josh shook his head, lips pursed. He wasn't trying to appear small anymore, but the slump of his shoulders alone was like an exposed wound to Ray's eyes. "It doesn't matter what happens; I've felt those things for you for a long time, and I didn't tell you because I thought it would make things weird. That maybe you'd be angry." He glanced up, long enough for Ray to see he looked like he was about to cry. "You *can* be angry, but you *can't* say it isn't true."

"Oh. Okay. I... I understand," Ray said, unable to bring himself to actually agree.

Josh nodded, looking calmer already. "Good," he declared. "There's something I wanted to ask you: did it change when I presented? Did you—I don't know, did you feel something?"

That, Ray could answer easily; it wasn't every day your best friend presented. He shook his head. "I was a beta; I didn't notice that you had presented at all. You know that," he added and even as he said the words he realised what they meant.

Josh wasn't speaking, but Ray knew him too well to miss his hopeful look. But it wasn't enough. Betas weren't meant to be consciously aware of the subtle scents that attracted alphas and omegas to each other—but that didn't mean they were completely unaffected. "What about you?"

Josh didn't answer immediately, taking a step away from the door but not closer to Ray, going towards the big window as his hand distractedly pulled at his own hair.

"When I presented... it changed things. But the same time, it didn't? I was attracted to you before that, and I was horny as hell right after, so... It was harder to stay away. But it wasn't because I could feel you'd be an omega *two years later*," he insisted, looking up to meet Ray's eyes briefly. Ray didn't speak, but his scepticism must have been clear in his expression. "I got off with Reese. That full moon. I was always with girls, I was always careful, but I lost control. It was my first full moon as an alpha, and I couldn't handle it."

"Reese?" Ray asked. He couldn't quite repress the shot of jealousy. Reese was an alpha now; why would Josh have chosen him instead of Ray?

Josh shrugged, looking a little uncomfortable. "Yeah, well, I thought if I stayed away from you, I'd be safe. He was there, and—"

"You left me behind," Ray said, remembering. "That night, I remember looking for you everywhere, because you always ran with me—"

"I'm sorry, Ray. You were too important."

"And then what? I presented and I wasn't anymore?"

"What? No! I was so worried about you, you know?" he said, gaze wandering about the room like he hadn't seen it a million times. "I knew you were an omega, obviously, but I was just so busy finding alphas we could trust that I kinda forgot that's why you needed them. And then I saw you in the hall and you looked..." Ray didn't need him to say it; if he'd looked half as bad as he'd felt, he must have been a sorry sight—and if anybody could see past his brave face, it'd be Josh. But Josh swallowed and finished anyway. "You looked awful, Ray. And they all went..." He paused, turning to look out the window. Ray couldn't even see his profile. He stiffened just remembering stepping into that hall in which most of the alphas of his pack had been eager to bend him over and shove it in him. It'd been the first time he'd been in the presence of an alpha he wasn't closely related to after he'd presented. He'd been fucking terrified, and they'd been... "They got so... excited," Josh added, sounding awkward.

"And you?" Ray dared to ask. It was an unforgivably stupid question to ask an alpha. Josh couldn't help...

But Josh wasn't just an alpha; he was Ray's best friend. "And all *I* wanted was to get you out of there. Away from..." He leaned against the frame and met Ray's eyes and Ray thought there were tears lurking in his beautiful hazel eyes. "I was glad you made a run for it."

"But you made me come back," Ray said. He didn't mean to sound accusatory but it was hard to keep it back. "Why didn't you... You could have told me then."

Josh winced, but then, as if bracing himself, he met Ray's eyes again. "I... I thought about it, but... Would you have believed me then? Right after you had presented? Right after I'd seen you as an omega for the first time? You were so angry I had *offered,* you punched me, Ray."

"Of course I was angry!" Ray snapped, stepping away from Josh because he wanted to step closer. He remembered how it'd felt to hit him, how *right* it'd been. But he also remembered that Josh couldn't hit him back. "How else was I supposed to feel? Doesn't mean I couldn't have listened to you."

Josh closed his eyes, then admitted in a gutted voice. "I thought if I told you what I felt; if you knew I really wanted you... It was selfish, but I thought you'd send me away. I couldn't bear it. I couldn't even *think* about leaving you with them."

"So you lied to me."

"I..." Josh started. "I didn't tell you the truth. I thought it was the right thing to do, if it meant I got to keep you safe that way."

"I see," Ray bit out with all the bitter disappointment of someone who expects little and gets even less. "Good thing me being an omega didn't change how you felt about me, right? It took you about five seconds to decide I didn't get to make my own decisions anymore."

Josh flinched. "I didn't think... I didn't think about you being an omega. I just thought about you being in a shitty situation and how proud you are. I was afraid you'd refuse my help—"

"I had the right to refuse!"

Josh met his eyes, looking like he was walking on burning coals as he did. "Yes."

"So you just—"

"I was selfish," Josh said, facing him, "because I love you."

But the words couldn't heal all wounds—no matter how long Ray had wanted to hear them. Josh had admitted his selfishness and excused it away in the same breath.

"Because you love me or because you couldn't bear for another alpha to fuck me instead of you?" Ray demanded, so bitterly furious his voice was like a blow.

Josh gasped and took a step back, flinching when his elbow hit the corner of the dresser.

They'd always spoken plainly to each other before, but they'd never talked about having sex with each other without generalising. They'd never talked about the fact that Josh fucked him on a regular basis, or about how that made Ray feel. It'd seemed safer that way, but now Ray saw that it was actually completely crazy. He'd been sleeping with the man for a year and he hadn't ever talked to him about it, never tried to negotiate or balance it out. They'd probably talked more about the rules of wrestling when they were ten than about what was okay to do with each other's bodies in bed.

Of course Josh had assumed Ray would prefer it if he bedded him as infrequently as possible.

"I *was* jealous," Josh admitted, voice growing darker with pain. "I couldn't *help* it. You were my... my best friend, and I was the one who'd wanted you forever, and I thought maybe you... And then it turned out maybe we could be together. But not really because your uncle insisted you were going to be First Omega of a new pack."

"But you still didn't fucking ask me what I wanted!" Ray snapped, so incensed he thought he might hit him again. Except that wasn't possible any longer, not now that Josh wasn't just an alpha but *Ray's* alpha. He shouldn't have done it anyway, it wasn't okay to hit people just because you were angry and Ray had never been prone to losing control—but the fact that he *couldn't*...

"No!" Josh screamed back. "I fucking didn't. I'm sorry, okay? I should have! But it happened so *fast*. I was trying to calm you down, and then the others were explaining... and you agreed to it and, I don't know, Ray. If you had asked me that day, I'd have gone with you anywhere you wanted."

But it hadn't even occurred to Ray to ask. There was no reason an omega needed more than one alpha. It was just a convention that male omegas were mated and bred by several since they were able to carry more pups.

They *could have gone*, he realised with dawning horror. He stared at Josh, swallowing compulsively as his heart started to race. The overlooked possibility felt like a betrayal he could never forgive, but not from Josh—from himself.

"No," his friend said, taking a hesitant step closer. "I'm sorry, don't..." He took hold of Ray's forearm, just loose enough that Ray could shake him off if he wanted. "Don't freak out. It's okay." He rubbed Ray's arm and brought him closer, taking hold of his elbows to support his weight as Ray's balance faltered. "Think about it: you'd have never been able to see your family again. You wouldn't have really wanted that, would you?"

Ray shook his head weakly, suddenly so weary his knees bent a little. Josh caught his weight more firmly and Ray leaned into him—took his strength as it was offered. He'd only glimpsed the possibility of freedom for an instant, but giving it up again was unbearable.

He let Josh lead him to the bed and fell on his back. His shirt felt scratchy against his sensitive nipples. He should probably just throw it away. Just get rid of everything that wasn't pure cotton and stop pretending he'd ever go back to normal. That there was a normal to go back to.

"Ray," Josh said with so much despair colouring his voice that Ray turned his head towards him. He was sitting on the edge bed, staring at Ray with worried eyes, body tense with his repressed need to touch Ray.

Ray didn't want Josh to be sad, but it was all abstract to him, an idea only. He felt numb, not unaware of the pain but separated from it.

He was about to tell Josh he was fine when his friend reached out and thumbed at his cheek. It was wet. He blinked, feeling the heaviness on his eyelashes. He was crying, he understood. His breathing was laboured too, a little too fast. He couldn't remember the last time he'd cried, but that only made it more real. His body telling his mind what he'd been incapable of seeing on his own. It was like breathing in after holding your breath too long—if you breathed in inside a volcano. It hurt, choking him with emotion too strong to be held in any longer and he curled up on his side, trembling and sobbing into the bedding.

He knew when he'd last cried, of course; it had been the day his dad had died.

And now... now Ray was dead. The person he'd been, the person he'd dreamed of becoming. He was gone forever.

Josh lay back next to him and put his arm around Ray's middle, uncaring of the tears and probably the snot as he brought Ray's head to his own chest to cradle. Ray let him. Ray needed him. It was nothing to be ashamed of; Josh needed him too.

They stayed like that for a while, until Ray felt like he truly couldn't breathe properly and tried to reach for a tissue. Josh held on for a moment longer before he made himself let go and passed them to Ray without being asked.

He was sitting up on the bed when Ray turned around, eyes irritated like he'd cried himself even though his face was dry.

"It wouldn't have worked," he told Ray. "I'm sorry I said anything. It was just a fantasy, not—"

"No, it's..." Ray swallowed. "It's fine. I... you just made me see something I've been trying not to see." He swallowed and blew his nose, trying to order his thoughts. "I guess I still thought there was a way back. No, not thought, exactly, but I felt like there had to be. But it's gone, and I'm fine now. I've seen it and I accept it. I'm fine."

"You don't have to be."

Ray pushed up onto his elbows to look at him and shook his head. It simply wasn't true. He sat up fully. "Yeah, I do," he said, "I thought I could just pretend and it'd be enough, but it's not. I *need* to let it all go. Being an alpha and going away to explore the world, and the world where you and me were together and we lived in the city in a shitty flat with smelly roommates."

Josh gave him a weak smile. "Isn't that the world we live in?"

Ray shook his head. "Please, Alec makes me a five-course meal for breakfast every day, and nothing can break without Gabriel making sure it's fixed on the same day."

"You deserve it," Josh said, leaning in and touching Ray's face gently again. "And you deserved better from me. I should have asked you, even if it meant you got angry at me. Even if meant you asked me to go," he added.

An omega could never take it back once he'd given himself to an alpha, but Josh sounded like the possibility of Ray telling him to go was still real and too painful to speak of.

That was all that Ray had needed to hear. It didn't erase his pain—nothing could do that—but it acknowledged it. There was no way for Josh to fix his past mistakes or the pain they'd caused Ray, much less fix Ray's own missteps. But he could admit that he'd been wrong. It was all it took: you admitted you had been wrong and then you had a chance in hell of not being wrong again, but most people had too much pride to take the easy way out. "It wasn't... I wasn't angry at you, not really. I shouldn't have hit you," he said, trying the high road himself.

Josh frowned at him, hands clenching in his lap to keep himself from touching Ray while he wasn't sure the touch would be welcome. "What do you mean?"

Ray shot him an incredulous look. "Can you imagine there was anyone else in the universe I wanted to see me as an omega less than you?" he asked, turning away to throw the tissue into the bin across the room. Supernatural reflexes and all, gravity wasn't on his side. The tissue fell halfway through.

"Oh, you really..." Josh stopped and Ray couldn't resist looking at his face. He was watching Ray right back.

He realised Josh's pulse was speeding only a moment after feeling his own thudding in his chest. It was odd, because he'd told Josh already and Josh had said it back. But something had changed now. The past was gone, but they were here.

Josh reached out so slowly, enough that the slowest of humans could have pulled away, to put his hand on top of Ray's on his lap. His palm was rough from work, but his expression was all tenderness and for a long moment Ray watched him back. He'd kissed Josh hundreds of times, but in that moment, he wanted to lean in more than anything. And he knew he couldn't.

Not after what they'd told each other. But he couldn't move away, either, not when for the first time since he'd become Josh's omega, he felt like they were okay. He pulled on Josh's hand until it was around his waist and leaned close for an embrace—as chaste as could be with the way they were sitting. But it didn't seem to matter. Josh held him back almost desperately, breathing heavily.

"You can do whatever you want," he promised. "We'll help you, make it work. You could go back to college or paint all day or... anything."

"I don't really know what I want," Ray admitted. How did you even begin to dream again after not just your future but your present disappeared from one day to the next?

"That's okay," Josh said, rubbing his back through his shirt. "You have time to figure it out."

Sergi was sound asleep on their shared bed, and Iesu was curled up in the armchair next to the window. Right next to the easel Ray had set up to sketch their lover. His eyes were on the man on the bed, but Iesu had his ear as soon as he decided to speak.

"Something's different about you. Since you talked to Josh, I think."

Ray pulled the pencil away from the drawing and turned to glare at his alpha. Iesu might have overheard some of their conversation—he was well-aware that they'd both raised their voices enough to be heard with *human* hearing—but that didn't mean he knew what Ray was thinking. Iesu kept watching Sergi, though, pretending not to notice.

"Didn't realise you were my shrink now," Ray said, doing his best to keep his voice even.

"So you admit you need one."

"Do I?" he asked, hoping against hope that his alpha would take the hint and let it be. He carefully put the pencil to the paper again, glanced at Sergi and traced a line that he immediately had to rub out.

Iesu was undeterred. "I'm just saying you've had a rough year, Ray. You could talk to someone about it, is all."

"I did talk to someone," Ray said, sighing. "Wasn't that what you wanted?"

"True," Iesu admitted raising his hands in defeat. "You figured it out with Josh. I'm glad, I just... I wondered if I could ask about it. I know I'm not Josh, but I care about you."

He hadn't figured out a thing with Josh, if anything, they'd tangled things up even further. But he was glad they'd talked anyway, at least now he didn't have to worry that Josh would notice how he felt. At least now when Josh kissed him too softly, he wouldn't have to pull back because he couldn't bear to be touched like that without knowing if it was an expression of real feeling. It was real.

It wasn't the only thing that was real, though, and maybe that was the only thing that Ray was sure about: he was an omega and his life had changed forever. He didn't want to talk about Josh, but he could tell Iesu that much, and maybe it'd be enough to get him to back off the rest.

He hesitated, then deliberately turned to the drawing and added a line to Sergi's elbow.

"I just realised there's no going back," he told Iesu. "It's obvious, but a part of me thought there would be a normal somewhere, that..." He trailed off, unsure of how to explain the wild, impossible hope he'd kept alive for so long.

"There *is* a normal," Iesu offered, "just not the one from before. It won't always be crazy, we'll settle. The betas will get here and we'll get hot meals on the table more often than not, and stop washing clothes twice because we never hung them up."

"I know."

"And football, and time to draw hot naked guys," Iesu added with his usual optimism.

Ray snorted, eyes flickering between the two men. "You're really gone on him, aren't you?"

Iesu met his eyes head-on. "Jealous?" he asked with a smirk.

"Obviously," Ray agreed, and extended a palm towards the sleeping man—dark skin sprawled on white sheets like something out of a dream.

Iesu barely muffled his laughter in time, but he knew there was nothing for Ray to be jealous of when it came to Sergi's body, naturally. His eyes were serious when he met Ray's. "Did you tell him?"

Ray looked away, biting his lip against the wolf's need to answer its alpha. He was okay with telling Iesu what he'd realised about himself, but not about Josh. He couldn't think of anything he wanted to discuss less than what he felt for Josh, or Josh for him. It was between them alone, a fragile new-born hope. He wasn't sure it'd live to see another day or what would become of it—but like an overzealous parent, he wanted nothing in its way, not even his own thoughts.

"Ray? What's wrong?"

"Direct question," Ray got out, willing to answer *that*.

"What? Really? But—" He bit down on the objection and said quickly. "You don't have to answer. Just if you want to."

Ray exhaled, shaky and tired all of sudden. "Please don't bring it up again," he requested. He managed to put the pencil down on the table instead of dropping it, but then he had to leave. He wasn't angry, exactly, but being given a direct order by one of his alphas always left him feeling unbalanced, like they'd suddenly yanked the floor from under feet. It was even worse when they'd done it without even noticing. For them, it was an accident; for Ray...

Iesu didn't try to stop him or follow, at least, so Ray had somewhere to go for a little quiet.

Chapter 8

Ray had called his uncle's wife, the first omega of lakeside Pack, and she'd assured him he was welcome to stop by with all of his alphas. But it was just Iesu and Josh who'd ended up going with him. Someone had to stay with the kids while Ray fetched the betas that had been meant to be supporting his newly formed pack since its beginnings. And most of them still had to go to work—Josh was the only one doing mostly night shifts. They'd taken the Jeep in case someone decided to drive back with them, but Ray didn't expect anybody to be *that* enthusiastic. For a beta to join a pack, its first omega or alpha had to approve and personally invite them, so it'd be very short notice indeed. And in any case, they didn't even have a room ready for them yet. Iesu had moved in with Sergi easily enough—their rooms had been next door to each other and Iesu was happy to live with only a suitcase worth of clothing—but they hadn't purchased the bunk beds or bedding.

Ray looked out the window, feeling his breath catch as they crossed over, and Josh glanced at him from the lake's seat. "You okay?" he asked. He'd become much more vocal about his concern since their conversation—it reminded Ray of how things had been before.

"Yeah, it's just... I can feel it. I can feel I'm in someone else's territory, it's..." He shrugged. He didn't mention that he had stopped feeling Alec and the pups back home when they'd crossed over, or that the wolf was already impatient to get back to them. "Weird."

"What does it feel like?" Iesu asked from the backseat.

"It's... I guess there's this pressure, like when someone's staring at you," Ray explained.

"Huh, well, I guess you can feel their first omega watching you," Iesu deduced. "That makes sense."

"Should we drive up to your mother's house?" Josh asked.

"Mariah said not to stand on ceremony," Ray said. "So yeah, let's just go for it. My mum might not be First Omega, but I don't want to piss her off."

"Plus she'll feed us," Iesu mused happily.

Ray turned to raise an eyebrow at him. "Are you not eating enough? Alec made a *rack* yesterday and you had like half a dozen eggs this morning."

It'd been their delayed celebration of the betas coming, so there had been almost too many side-dishes to fit on their table. And with Alec's approval, they'd let the pups try their teeth on actual bones. Jamie had taken to it quite enthusiastically, which Ray hoped meant he'd stop resisting Ray's attempts to stop breastfeeding him.

Iesu shrugged, boyishly charming. "What can I say? I'm a growing boy."

Ray snorted. "What about your family? Did you tell them you'd be there at a particular time?"

"Nah," Iesu said, "I said we'd be around and I'd give them a ring sometime today. You might recognize some of them from our footie team back when we played you."

"Oh?"

"Irina is a goalie. She's pretty obsessed with Man United, too, and just football in general. I had to promise we'd have matches before she'd think about joining us."

Ray swallowed at the thought. For a moment, he remembered running after a ball, his body sure and true, and then he straightened in his seat and the strangeness of his body pulled him sharply from the memory. He licked his lips, glancing out the window and away from Iesu. "And how old is she?"

"Don't worry, Ray, she's a beta. She's thirty already, nobody presents that late."

"I'm not sure about Marisa," he admitted. "She's so young..."

Josh put a hand on his knee and squeezed. "Worst case scenario, she'll present in a year or two and you get to have your sister around. Wouldn't that be nice anyway?"

Ray wasn't that close to Marisa, but she was still his little sister. He wasn't sure he wanted her around if she presented omega. If she had to go through what he was going through himself. But, of course, it wouldn't be like that; female omegas bonded to a single alpha and it was no worse than marriage or partnership was for betas, really. Most omega girls he'd known growing up had chosen their own alpha, too, and in his pack, Ray could make sure nobody tried to order them around or influence them...

No, that wasn't the reason he wasn't sure he wanted Marisa living with them. Even with the alphas planning to build another set of rooms with their own bathroom and with Iesu's room freed for the betas, it'd still mean very close quarters.

She would see it all. She would witness what he'd become.

If it was hard with Josh, he couldn't imagine his family starting to see him as an omega.

Marisa wouldn't think less of him for it. Werewolf girls grew up with the very real possibility of becoming omegas and even betas often ended up having children. His mother had understood that it upset him, but she hadn't pitied him for it. For her, being an omega had meant marrying the man she loved and forming a family with him.

It was the way it was meant to be. Even if you were a man. But nobody had told Ray or his friends that it might be *them* who became that, who lived that life. Ray had thought about male omegas only in the context of other people. If he was perfectly honest, he'd found them fascinating but disturbing.

It was meant to be normal since it was natural. But it'd never felt that way, and it still didn't. He didn't know if it ever could.

But he was just being selfish again. His pack needed betas, and it didn't really matter in the short term if they didn't stay betas. And Marisa had offered, and Ray knew how great she was with kids. He couldn't afford to be squeamish, and after everything he'd learned to accept in his new life, it'd have been ridiculous to baulk at having his sister around to witness it.

He'd sent Nicholas and the other alphas away, that certainly was worth a little familial discomfort.

"Ray?" Josh asked. Ray looked at him. "We are here," his friend said gently.

It was true. Josh was parked in the same spot he'd used for years to drop Ray off and pick him up. Ray turned to the house like a flower to the sun. It didn't look smaller, even though it was pretty small compared to the new place the alphas had built. It looked the same, a little ragged around the edges because nobody had given it a fresh coat of paint since his dad had died—Ray could have, he realised, but back when he'd lived there it had never crossed his mind—but cosy and familiar.

He couldn't think back to the comfort and the scent of his closest family and their life together, though. All he could remember was huddling in his room as his skin started to itch, as the thoughts that felt foreign started racing through his mind. It'd been barely a couple of days from the moment he'd woken up changed to the day when he'd been taken away, but it felt like the whole place was soaked in the memory.

Ray made himself get out of the car, and Josh and Iesu followed. Josh was reminding Iesu of everybody's names. Ray was pretty sure his friend knew he needed to be left alone, if only by not being spoken to for a while. But then they were at the front door and he had to knock.

His little brother opened the door without asking who it was and without putting the chain on. But Ray didn't have the heart to shout at him for it, though, not when Glen's face split into a smile at the sight of him and he threw himself at Ray directly. He caught him, surprised by the weight of him. It couldn't have been that long, could it? But Glen was five—he'd been born not long after their father had passed—and even a short period of time could make a big difference. Ray picked him up and he buried his nose into Ray's neck, probably reassuring himself that Ray was okay by smelling him. Ray held him close for a long moment. Not long ago, Glen had been as close to his own child as anybody. Ray had thought he'd raise him until he was able to care for himself, and now...

But he was blocking the doorway and letting in the cold—once upon a time, he'd have scolded himself for that. He made himself step inside and heard Josh and Iesu following and closing the door. Anna and Harry were waiting inside, looking eager but unsure. Ray saw his sister's eyes flicker down his body and had to stop himself from moving Glen so his little body would cover his own middle. It was stupid, he looked normal now; what did he have to hide?

"Can I hug you?" Anna checked, eyes big as pools. She'd thrown herself into his arms the first time he'd visited, belly round but small, and got a scolding from their mother for it.

"Of course," Ray said and soon he was trapped in a group hug that mostly involved his middle and legs even when he hunched over. Josh got a similar treatment a moment later, except by Glen, who stayed glued to Ray's hip.

"This is Iesu, my mate," he explained to his siblings when they had calmed down enough to listen.

"But Josh is your mate," Anna objected with a frown. She was only eight and there weren't that many omegas around with more than one alpha.

"Yes," Josh intervened, "and so is Iesu. A person can have more than one mate."

Ray shot him a grateful look, but that was all he could manage at the moment. It was a bit too much to be back in a place where he'd been happy and free. Where *they* had been happy and free, because Josh had spent as much time in this house as Ray. Just like Ray had stayed at his. Josh's father had joked about officially adopting Ray once, and now... Well, now they were in-laws, he supposed. He hadn't even talked to Josh's family since the bonding and he'd barely heard *Josh* speak of them. He made himself promise to ask about it later, about all of their families.

Harry didn't seem sure about the explanation, but Ray spoke up before he could ask anything else. "Where are Marisa and TJ?"

"Oh, they went shopping. Glen is getting a real bed so mum needed help," his brother explained. "And I'm in charge."

Anna shot their brother an unimpressed look, but she didn't try and argue. Ray was impressed with her restraint. His sister was sweet but a complete rebel without a cause—both Ray and his mother had learned early on that she needed to be coaxed, not commanded. "I see. Shouldn't you be offering us tea, then?" he teased.

Harry's caught expression made Iesu laugh by his side. But it did the trick and got them all moving towards the living area. Ray curled up with Glen on one of the sofas and Josh sat Anna down at the other end so she could stay close to Ray without appearing clingy.

Harry had insisted on getting the tea himself and managed decently, even if the biscuits were all mixed up and the milk had apparently run out. It'd always been Ray reminding others to buy it, it seemed they still tended to forget if he didn't.

Just then, his mother and the older kids had got back. His mum abandoned the shopping on the floor and went straight for Ray, taking him into her arms without even giving him time to let go of her youngest child. With her scent surrounding him and her arms holding him up, Ray felt, for a moment, like he'd let go of the weight he now carried. He managed, maybe because of the little boy heavy at his side, to hold it back. He was First Omega of his pack now; he couldn't burst into tears at the slightest provocation.

"Oh, Ray," she said, smiling widely and looking him up and down. "You look good."

Ray shrugged, uncomfortably aware that Josh and Iesu could hear every word. He glanced at Glen. "Hey, sweetie, can you be good for me and go sit with Harry for a bit?"

Glen didn't look like he could, his little hands closed harder on Ray's clothes and he shook his head. Then a voice spoke from behind them.

"What about me, Glen?" Josh asked. He had a kind, sweet expression on his face that suited him perfectly. It was exactly who Josh was. It was exactly why Ray... "What about I make you fly like a plane?"

Glen paused. "Really high?"

"Of course," Josh agreed. Glen was already laughing hard and high by the time Ray dragged his mum out of the room.

"**I**s everything alright?" she asked the moment they were alone.

Ray frowned. "What? Yes, of course, why..."

"Well, we heard some rumours about some alphas in your territory..."

"Oh." Ray looked away. "Yeah, they came, but... well, they're gone. It wasn't a big deal. They wanted to... they wanted to become part of the pack, but I said no. So that's done."

"And they thought you would agree?" his mum asked indignantly. "With five alphas already! Honestly, alphas are quite clueless... Well, never mind that. Soon you'll have some betas. I don't know about the others, but at least your sister is going with you."

"Um, is that okay?" Ray asked timidly. It was the main reason he'd wanted to be alone with her.

His mum seemed baffled. "Is what okay?" she asked, hands reaching for scattered clothes and folding them on the dresser. Ray was pretty sure she didn't know she was doing it. The house wasn't any messier than when he'd left, but it was still... busy. You could tell there were a lot of kids around and that the adults weren't quite keeping up.

"Me taking Marisa away from you."

"You are not *taking* her, Ray!" His mum paused to shoot him an indignant look. "She volunteered, she wants to go!"

"But don't you need her?" Ray insisted, glancing about.

His mum didn't seem to follow his train of thought. "Me?" she asked sounding amused, "Oh, no, I'll be fine. TJ's been a lot of help lately, and Harry and Anna are in school all day. It's mostly Glen, really."

"But it's just... she's..."

"No," his mother interrupted, "don't even think to say that. She is your sister and she wants to help you. I want her to help you. You took care of all of us for a long time, Ray. It's time you let us help you now."

He hesitated. "You don't think she's an omega?"

She shrugged. "I don't know, and neither do you. But if she is, I know she will be safe with her big brother looking after her," she added. And was that regret in her tone? She'd tried to be cheerful when his uncle had chosen his mates for him, and even later when he'd been bred by them. She didn't sound so happy now. He wondered if she was so keen on Marisa going to him because she felt like she hadn't done enough to help him. But he needed the help too badly to question it, and he wasn't sure he could tell her she'd done enough without his pulse betraying him. He knew she'd done what she could, but he'd wanted more. And maybe he should have been used to it; there was only one of her and six of them and that meant that even when she did her best, it often wasn't enough. It didn't mean she didn't love him.

"She will," Ray said after a long pause. He didn't know how to reassure her, not without bringing up his suspicions—and if he was wrong, it'd make her think he thought she was responsible.

She nodded, seemingly satisfied, but then added, "And you will both come for a visit soon, won't you?"

"Yes, of course, and Marisa can come anytime, it's not far..."

"Ray," she said in a strained voice and took hold of his hands in hers. "I want to see you. I understand you needed... time. But we won't ask a thing. Just come and eat, let me play with my grandchildren. That's all. Glen misses you dreadfully. We all do."

Ray stared at their hands. "I didn't mean—"

"No," she shushed him. "Of course not. It was a shock. I understand, but... things are going well, aren't they? You've got your colour back and your mates care about you. Anybody can see that much."

Ray swallowed. He knew they cared about him, that they were trying, each in their own way, to makes things easier for him. They'd kept him from having to accept a terrible deal and they helped with the babies as much as the need for breastfeeding permitted.

He cared for them as well. It was just that not long ago he'd imagined a life with a partner he loved, someone he could grow to love before... before he said yes forever. Knowing he was stuck, how could he know that what he was feeling for them was anything but the natural fondness one developed for anyone who was kind and was always close? He didn't know how to make the story fit. They hadn't had a first date—or any dates at all. They hadn't kissed at first, passionate or sweet, and then made-out for a bit before moving on to the main event, or deciding to stop and take things slow.

It was all backwards. He didn't remember his first heat clearly, but he knew Gabriel had fucked him before he'd ever kissed him. It'd been the first time he'd done anything with a man. He wasn't sure it mattered that much that he'd always *wanted* to.

But his mother wasn't wrong. He was finding his way somehow, with Iesu's impromptu movie marathons, and Josh curling up with the babies, and Alec always making sure Ray ate enough and obsessively monitoring the babies' diet. It was the little things, really, that would have added up to more, to companionship, to family... to love.

The same things he'd stopped giving his own family.

"I will come," he promised his mother. "I will bring them soon; we can have a barbecue."

She didn't thank him, but he didn't need her to say the words.

Irina was a looker. She had her cousin's tanned colouring and dark eyes, but the same long-lashed and heavy-lidded look that Iesu made look laid-back was full of cynicism on her face.

"You're the omega," she said dubiously. Ray realised she could probably tell he found her attractive. His face was burning, but he made himself meet her eyes.

"Yes, and you must be Irina. Iesu said we played you last season."

She scowled. "You didn't play *me*, I was injured. I remember that game, complete mess. Iesuvel..." She sighed and seemed to stop herself from continuing with an effort. "Well, let's say I hope he's better with other types of balls." She shrugged.

Iesu snorted and Josh made a noise like he'd choked on air while Ray simply stared. Iesu's hand on his arm startled him. He offered Ray a sweet apologetic smile. "Forgot to mention Irina's got a mouth on her, didn't I?"

"Yes," Ray agreed, glancing between them.

"Don't worry," Irina added, "I know how to keep it PG in front of the kids."

Ray watched her for a moment. A strong, opinionated woman who could more than hold her own. She was a beta so she'd never lead her pack, but that didn't mean she couldn't rise through the ranks. "Do you like kids?"

She nodded. "Yeah, they talk sense, no plotting or hints or anything. They tell it like they see it. And sometimes it's complete nonsense, but then at least you know and you can explain or whatever. Or they can explain."

"Plotting?" Ray asked, confused. His uncle ran a big pack but he hadn't noticed any undue tensions, nothing beyond the everyday conflicts of people living in close proximity and sharing resources.

"Irina's a bit of a drama queen, she doesn't like to attend pack functions and make nice."

Irina glared at Iesu. "I don't like to go around to alphas' houses and show my belly, you mean."

Iesu shrugged. "All you have to do is smile at their jokes and eat their food, and they're happy."

She snorted. "I'm sure that's why you got out as fast as you did..."

"Well," Iesu replied smiling, "I didn't say we weren't a better deal, just that it's not that bad here."

Once upon a time, Ray would have defended his uncle and his pack. But this wasn't his pack anymore. His uncle's blood still ran through his veins, but Ray wasn't so sure that mattered that much to the alpha. He'd said yes to the betas, but only when Ray had asked for them, and—he now realised—he'd never checked on Ray after assigning the alphas to him.

"Okay," he said and the others must have understood because they stopped chatting and turned to look at him. "Okay," he repeated, "I would like you to come. If you're okay with sharing a room for a bit. Gabriel said the new wing..."

Irina waved him off. "Sharing's fine. I'll help with the building, too."

Ray gave her a smile and extended his hand. "Welcome to our pack."

"**M**arisa, I just want to be sure you offered for the right reasons—"

"Look, I probably can't have kids," she cut him off.

"What?" Ray said. "How...?"

"Do you really want the gory details?" his sister asked bitterly. "I'm pretty sure, and mum... she agrees. So, yeah, just... I want to help you, but I want it for my own reasons, too."

"But maybe it doesn't have to be like that," Ray objected, "Maybe it can be, I don't know, fixed. Maybe if you talked to Alec—"

"Alec?" she repeated. "Ray, do you really think I haven't talked to every doctor in every pack in the county? No offence to your mate, but he's barely graduated, and all the doctors say the same thing: we don't know shit about our own biology because it's too hard to study it in secret."

It was the same thing Alec had said. It was the reason he and his alphas had been guessing about how to keep Ray from getting pregnant. Marisa must have misunderstood his defeated expression because she added, "I'm fine with it. Some betas can't have kids, it's not... it's not the end of the world. Doesn't mean I can't look after them and love them just the same."

Ray snorted. "How fucking unfair does the world have to be that I get to have exactly what you want when it's the last thing I want?"

"Very," Marisa answered, eyes dark and much older than her age, "but I'm not taking it lying down. I'll carve my own life out of everything that's thrown at me. And so should you. Take my help, take mum's, take what you need, the world isn't going to hand you anything on a silver plate."

Ray swallowed, then nodded. "Okay," he told her. "Come, please come."

"I will," his sister said. Ray thought it was the first time he truly understood her. "You'll be sorry when I ban take-away, but I'm great at making them burp, so all in all, you are better off."

Ray laughed, reminded of passing Glen to her when he couldn't get him to burp himself. She had a gift with babies he could never hope to equal, no matter the two extra years of practice he had on her—much less the fact that they were his own children.

"I think I will be."

Chapter 9

"Nicholas," Ray said, staring a little.

He'd felt strangers in his territory, but he'd assumed it was the new betas or someone from his former pack. The betas wouldn't be officially part of the pack until the full moon, when Ray would symbolically welcome them in a ceremony that he was grateful was completely lacking in anything remotely sexy. And since the betas' arrival, they'd got a lot more visits, as if the old pack people had realised they hadn't really lost them simply because they were across the lake. Iesu's family had been over just the day before, curious to see where their wayward son had gone and where Irina would be settling. Because they'd been invited by a pack member, nobody had felt the need to announce themselves to Ray in any way before reaching the front door. That had been fine by him. Until now.

"Hello, Raymond," Nicholas smiled. There was no trace of resentment or anger on his face, and Ray couldn't smell anything either. "We are on our way back home; thought I'd stop by."

Ray blinked at him. It was true he had invited Nicholas into pack territory in the first place, but it had been obvious to him the offer was rescinded once he had withdrawn his invitation to join the pack. He was sure that anybody else would understand how awkward the situation was, but Nicholas seemed to be genuinely unaware. "It's not—"

A pup bumped into his leg and clung there, forcing Ray to turn to pick them up. Clara, of course, their runaway. By the time he straightened, Nicholas's friends were waiting behind him. They had probably stayed out of sight to avoid startling him.

"Just... come in for a cuppa," Ray offered, already distracted. He did not have time for social visits, but he still felt bad about rejecting Nicholas; he could spare them half an hour. He could probably find some biscuits from the big shopping trip Iesu and Alec had gone on not that long ago, assuming nobody had found the ones Ray had stashed behind the kitchen rolls. Marisa had threatened him with forbidding them from eating fast food, but Ray was actually looking forward to someone organizing the practical stuff he and his alphas never quite seemed to have the time for.

She had come over early. The other betas weren't quite done settling their affairs and organizing rides to work, so they just stopped by some afternoons a week. Irina's mother had driven her over the day before with a truly impressive number of boxes that, to go by the labels, contained mostly football memorabilia. Ray had no idea where she thought she'd put it, but since the boxes hadn't been left in sight, he supposed it was none of his businesses.

She was gone again today and wouldn't be coming back until Friday. To be fair, they only had bunk beds in Iesu's old room for them to sleep in. The alphas were using every spare moment to work on the new wing where the betas would live.

They had walls already up, but that was all that could be said for the new bedrooms, and the toilet wouldn't get done until they could get a specialist to come in and install the sewage. Ray'd had the foresight of insisting on two full bathrooms in the main house, but that was the bare minimum they needed for the people already living there.

"Oh, well, this looks much nicer already," Nicholas commented as they walked into the living area. Marisa had gone through it that morning so it was tidier than usual, but Ray just shot his guest a smile. His sister looked tense, so he shook his head at her and smiled in reassurance. Anybody would be startled to have six alphas walk into their territory, of course.

"Just take a seat, I'm going to make tea."

He'd barely put the kettle on the stand when he felt a presence behind him. He turned to find Nicholas in the doorway. He must have followed Ray. The kitchen was a good corridor away from the living room, facing the back of the house. They'd decided to do it that way so both of the family rooms could get a lot of sunlight, a scarce commodity even in southern England.

"Hey," Ray said, "Did I forget to—?"

"Yes," Nicholas interrupted, there was no trace of his easy smile. "You forgot your promise to me."

Ray took a cautious step back. "I did not forget. I withdrew it."

"And you can just do that?" Nicholas demanded. "Take it back like it meant nothing? Like your word means nothing?"

"Nicholas," Ray tried again, "I made a mistake, and I'm really sorry that I hurt you, but—"

"Are you sorry enough to make up for it?" Nicholas interrupted, eyes bright. Ray's mind raced. Was there something he could have done? Some way in which the rejection could have stung less?

"I..." He swallowed. "Sure, if I can do anything..."

"Go through with it," the alpha said immediately. "Go through with it and we'll call it a holiday me and the guys took."

Ray stared, then made himself speak, "I can't do that, you know I can't..."

Nicholas's face darkened in fury and he took another step towards Ray. They were in Ray's territory, in his own home, but Nicholas was angry enough to make his alpha will overwhelming, and he'd caught Ray unprepared. His back bumped against the kitchen counter as the alpha caged him in.

His wolf was torn; it recognized Nicholas as a strange alpha, someone who had no right to touch Ray at all, but it remembered that Ray had let Nicholas kiss him. And when an alpha tried to dominate, an omega's first instinct was to submit. He was still standing in his own kitchen, paralysed with uncertainty and guilt, when Nicholas leaned in and roughly took hold of his face, forcing him to stay in place as his tongue invaded Ray's mouth with possessive delight.

Ray struggled weakly and then harder, but Nicholas was stronger than him. Even when Ray's wolf got with the program, it wasn't enough. He thought about biting him, but attacking an alpha was hard and attacking someone stronger than you who was already angry didn't seem wise. Nicholas only pulled back when he decided to, leaving Ray a panting mess and not stepping back from his body, heavy erection pressing against Ray's belly as he leaned into him.

"Let me—" Ray started.

"Shush now," Nicholas ordered, low and heavy. "We're going for a walk, we need to talk this over."

"I'm not—" Ray tried again, but Nicholas simply tightened his hands on Ray's hips and leaned closer still.

"You are going to be very quiet as we leave so my guys don't think anything's wrong," Nicholas warned as his hands patted down Ray's body. "We left them holding your little ones, remember? Anybody can have an accident and drop a kid that age wrong. Werewolves or not, a broken neck is a broken neck."

Ray jerked so hard in his hold that Nicholas had to struggle to keep him in place. "You *bastard*, if you fucking touch them—"

"I've got you by the bollocks, Raymond," Nicholas replied, silky and pleased and, as if he couldn't resist, squeezed Ray's arse. "And I know you like it. I know you don't have a real alpha, just these poor sods who follow you around and feel sorry for you."

Ray stomach twisted in revulsion, but he kept his mouth shut. He'd thought he could reason with Nicholas, up to a point. But an alpha who would threaten pups... Ray had to *do* something, there had to be something... He concentrated on listening to the pups, and he could hear enough to identify laughter and giggling. Marisa hadn't left, of course, but none of his alphas had come over like he'd almost hoped. They must have been busy with the work and if they were drilling, they probably wouldn't hear anything short of a commotion. And Ray had let these strangers into their house. He hadn't even warned his alphas that they'd come into their territory.

How could he have been so stupid? Not that it mattered. It was his mistake and he'd pay for it. He'd pay for it again and again if it was necessary. He'd put his body between his pack and danger, even if it meant he didn't make it back alive.

"Okay," he told Nicholas, "we can talk."

Not that he thought Nicholas wanted to kill him. His intentions were far more sinister than death; Ray would be alive to suffer the consequences.

Nicholas snorted. "Very generous of you. Now move, no sudden moves because *I promise you*; they are all sitting with a pup in their laps by now."

He let Ray step away from the counter and towards the back door. Ray's eyes darted around for some kind of weapon, or at least his mobile. But it was probably still plugged in on his bedside table, where he'd taken to keeping it while he fed the babies. Even if his mother or siblings wanted him, they called him on the landline, secure in the knowledge that Ray felt too uncomfortable leaving his territory to even go to the cinema in town.

Not that having his mobile would have helped, Ray could swear Nicholas didn't blink once until the door was closed behind them. The kitchen was far enough away that nobody would hear the door closing unless they were listening. And even if Marisa got suspicious about the absence of tea, she wouldn't leave the pups with strangers to check on Ray. Ray wouldn't have done it either, not for the world, except... Except he'd been stupid enough to think that a couple weeks of sharing meals and conversation meant he knew these men. Knew Nicholas, at least.

Nicholas took hold of his forearm, his grip like a vice, and started leading Ray towards the tree line. He wanted them out of sight as soon as possible, Ray realised. Not that it helped him much. If he tried to run, Nicholas could easily return to the house and even if Ray was faster, he'd have no backup once he got there.

No, he had to give his alphas time to notice his absence. Hopefully, after a while, Nicholas's friends would figure out they had to get out of the house before Ray's alphas decided to ask them where Ray was. And then... Well, he hoped he'd know what to do.

He looked up and stopped in his tracks, jostling Nicholas, who turned around to glare at him. "Where are you taking me?" he asked, not caring that he was being defiant. They were at least a mile from the house by now.

"Away," Nicholas replied firmly. "Come."

Ray pushed down his terror. He hadn't needed to ask; Nicholas was taking him out of his territory, to a place where he'd not only be easy to subjugate physically but would lose his ability to locate others in the land as well. If he had little hope in his own land, outside it...

"Wait," he begged, resisting Nicholas's renewed pull. "Let's just talk. I know—"

Nicholas shoved him, hard enough to send Ray sprawling onto the ground, hands coming down hard to keep his face from smashing into a tree trunk.

"Talk?" the alpha asked him, voice dripping with disdain. "What good is it to talk to a lying bitch like you? You'd just say whatever you thought I wanted to hear, then stab me in the back."

Ray looked up at him, shocked to the core. He didn't know why but he couldn't quite believe Nicholas would really be capable of this.

"I didn't lie," he insisted. He knew it was useless, but he hoped Nicholas could hear the truth anyway. "I *changed my mind*."

"You went back on your word," Nicholas gritted out. Ray remembered he'd praised Ray for being honest once, but apparently, honesty only worked when the truth never changed. "Now shut the fuck up before I fuck you right here."

Ray stared, not standing and not saying anything else. He'd known, of course, but... His hearing focused on the distance, trying to catch anything that would give him an advantage. But it was useless, they were far from everything, definitely too far from the house, and it'd been a quarter of an hour at most. He had to keep going. He had to risk it because he couldn't risk letting this madman close to his children. No matter what. He pushed to his knees, then his feet, and Nicholas stepped forward and took hold of his shirt by the neck to drag him along as he increased his pace.

He was hurting Ray's neck by forcing him to stoop, but Ray kept his mouth shut about it. His neck didn't matter, only that he let enough time pass before he tried to get away.

By the time they reached the border of Ray's land, Nicholas had been on the phone with his men twice. They hadn't said much of anything, although Ray heard Nicholas's guy passing instructions on to Marisa that supposedly came from Ray. Her voice had sounded calm, relaxed and friendly.

They were okay, but the implication was clear: they would only be okay as long as Nicholas didn't call to say otherwise.

Ray couldn't leave.

It was not physically painful to cross over, but it itched and it pulled. There was no first omega in this wild territory to feel watching over him, but everything in him, wolf and human, demanded that he return to his family. He knew they were still okay; he'd been able to feel them just before the connection stretched beyond his power.

He stumbled, and only Nicholas's grip kept him upright. "There, now you're free," the alpha told him.

Ray didn't answer. He kept walking, letting Nicholas's loose hold on him guide his steps.

He did not mean to get so lost in his thoughts that Nicholas could push him to the ground with barely any effort. And he fought him when it happened, twisting, and clawing, and spitting every word his mum had taught him not to repeat. But Nicholas was both heavier and in better shape than him, not having spent the last months sleeping less and worrying more than he should. Not to mention rarely leaving the house. He was like a boulder on top of Ray, his knees bracketing Ray's hips and keeping him down easily. Ray gritted his teeth and tried yanking his wrists out of the alpha's hold, but all Nicholas had to do was lean forward to keep him pinned. He was grinning, and he was hard.

He thought it was a game, Ray realised. He was going to rape him and he wouldn't hesitate even for a moment because he didn't believe Ray meant it.

"Stop," he pleaded, "Please stop, it's not you... I can't have any more alphas—"

Nicholas leaned down and kissed him, shoving his tongue into Ray's mouth while Ray struggled to breathe through it. It distracted Ray enough that he wasn't prepared at all for the hand going for his zipper. It was down in a flash, then back up slamming Ray's forearm down again as he tried to claw at the alpha. He managed to scratch him, but the alpha didn't give any sign that he'd noticed.

"Stay," he ordered Ray, eyes glowing in the falling light of the sun. The wolf cowered inside him, too confused by the situation, too lost out of his territory, to really understand the alpha was a threat. Nicholas ground against him without looking away and, to Ray's horror, the omega wolf reacted and showed his neck.

Eyes open to the rapidly darkening sky, Ray saw the moon directly above. It was almost full. The wolf would be gaining power over Ray the higher the full moon climbed in the sky, and the wolf seemed to have accepted a strange alpha was still an alpha...

He must have lost himself for a moment, spellbound by the call of the goddess, because the next thing he knew, Nicholas was ripping his jeans, neatly slashing through the crotch and legs with his sharp claws. Ray's underwear didn't fare any better and it was only when Nicholas got between his legs that Ray's brain caught on again.

The wolf was ready to submit, but the human would keep fighting. Ray twisted to the side and got to his knees, taking advantage of the fact that Nicholas had been forced to let go of his hands to pull his clothes off. Still from the ground, he aimed a kick at the advancing alpha. His bare foot connected with Nicholas's side and he got a grunt of pain for his trouble, but that was all. He was too close to have enough leverage. Nicholas's hand, still half claws, closed painfully around the bone of his ankle and gave a sharp tug, sending Ray tumbling onto his back once more. He was fast enough to claw at the alpha's arm before Nicholas pushed his whole weight on top of him, flattening him to the ground and forcing all the air from his lungs. He could smell blood next to his nose as Nicholas used the hand to push Ray down, but it was just a shallow wound.

Nicholas was still hard as a rod against Ray's now bare stomach. The remains of his trousers were half tangled on his legs and his shirt had ridden up during the struggle.

"Stop," Nicholas hissed into his ear and the wolf obeyed, freezing.

Ray got hold of himself again and answered, "You stop. I don't want this. You are no—"

But he didn't manage to finish because Nicholas lifted his knee and rubbed it against Ray's groin. The reaction was instantaneous, Ray's cock started to harden. Nicholas laughed.

"Sure you don't," he said with relish and used a hand to hold Ray's face in place for a kiss. Part of Ray wanted to bite him, but he wasn't sure he could force the wolf to do it, and what he truly wanted was something that would get him free. He let Nicholas have his mouth, mind racing for options.

"I bet you're wet for me," the alpha murmured, abandoning Ray's mouth to kiss his neck instead.

And Ray was, just like any omega would be when an alpha wanted him ready. He'd never before believed he was made for an alpha to mount. But as despair took over and his body burned with Nicholas's desire, he did. Nicholas rubbed his clothed knee against Ray's bare cock and balls. Ray keened, in desperation and pain at the feeling of the rough cloth against his sensitive genitals.

"Oh, yeah," Nicholas said happily. "You're gagging for it, aren't you?"

"'m not," Ray bit out between gasps for air. He felt like he was burning up, like he would explode. He was scared and wanted to run away and he... No, *he* didn't want Nicholas, it was just his body reacting to an alpha.

Nicholas's fingers pushed into him roughly, too fast and too many and Ray's back arched as he strained to get away. Nobody had been this rough with him before, not even during heat. But even if the wolf didn't force him to submit, he couldn't move far enough; Nicholas's fingers slid into his slick passage with ease. Nicholas grunted, rubbing his cock against Ray's thigh. He was holding Ray's wrists too tightly with his other hand, tightly enough that it was useless no matter how much Ray tried to separate them. Tightly enough that it felt like he wasn't getting enough blood to his fingers.

"Oh." Nicholas sighed. His knee was digging into Ray's hip and keeping him from rolling away, "You don't need to be prepared. You're just *ready*," he said in wonder. He pulled his fingers out, leaving Ray aching and uncomfortable but momentarily free.

Ray took the chance to roll away, dislodging Nicholas's knee with the force of his movement. He was immediately dragged back and shoved face first into the ground. Hands came down on his wrists even as Nicholas's body covered his once again, this time perfectly aligned. His hard cock found Ray's hole before Ray even had a chance to get his face off the dirt. And then he was in him, and going deeper, deep enough it felt like it was never going to end. Ray's legs were pushed aside so Nicholas could shove even deeper. Ray tried to arch, to twist, even as he choked on the dust his own face had stirred up. But it was no use, he was impaled on the alpha's hard dick and trapped by the alpha's full weight. Now that Nicholas had him, the only movements Ray was capable of did nothing but intensify the alpha's pleasure.

Nicholas was groaning loudly in his ear as his cock split Ray open again and again, rutting hard and merciless, completely ignoring Ray's struggles and pleads to stop.

"You are so good," he murmured in Ray's ear. "Feel so good. So wet, and ready, and desperate for me to give it to you."

"No..." Ray gasped out, even as the next thrust forced him to scramble to keep from falling forward again. Nicholas wasn't allowing him to lift his chest more than a few inches off the ground and it took all his concentration to keep his elbows locked in place to be able to breathe. And then it got worse: Nicholas hitched his hips up with a sharp tug and the next push felt suddenly good, lighting up something in Ray that made him shudder with lust.

"No!" he screamed. "Stop!"

Nicholas must have heard something in his voice because he did, still buried in Ray, and then he pushed in slowly again. Ray clenched around his girth, unable to control his battered muscles.

"Oh, sweetheart, you're too good to be true," Nicholas murmured in wonderment, and Ray wanted to tear his eyes out with his nails even as his wolf trembled at the praise.

When Nicholas pulled out, Ray was so shocked that for a moment he didn't react. But no matter how dazed his wolf was, *Ray* hadn't forgotten what was really happening here. He rolled to the side and jumped to his feet, kicking off the remains of his jeans as he turned to run. He heard Nicholas laughing behind him, but all he cared about was getting back to his own territory. The ground was littered with twigs, his thighs were slick with fluid and his hole still hurt. Ray wished he could shift and run as a wolf, but he could hear Nicholas close behind. A second might make all the difference.

And then the ground seemed to disappear from under his feet and he hit it hard, sprawling and skidding against the piled up autumn vegetation. It took a moment for his ears to stop ringing, and by then Nicholas already had hold of his legs and was flipping him over onto his back.

"Look what a mess you have made," he told Ray sweetly as he cleaned dirt from his face. Ray could feel tears prickling at his eyes, but he blinked, refusing to shed them. He'd once given up on the idea of choosing his own mates instead of letting his uncle choose for him and now he knew how right he'd been, but it was too late. He'd let Nicholas get close, and now...

He didn't struggle against Nicholas's hold on his wrists, not even when he used just one hand again. There was no point in fighting it, Nicholas had already proven he could take what he wanted and there was nothing Ray could do. And he was in so much pain, his whole torso was scratched up and his right side throbbed where he'd hit a big rock one of the times he'd fallen.

"There you go," Nicholas said and pushed Ray's right knee back against his chest so he could hook it over his own shoulder. Ray wanted to pull away, but his leg didn't move.

He could feel himself growing slicker in preparation against the hardness being pressed between his buttocks. The wolf, he understood, even in his daze. It was the wolf who was surrendering. When the moon was high, it was the wolf who was in charge. It didn't matter that it wasn't full yet, not when Ray was untethered from his pack: hurt, alone, and helpless. Ray watched as the alpha arranged his limbs to give himself access. It wasn't like heat at all. During heat he'd been pliant, sleepy, and so desperate it'd hurt; now he didn't feel anything. His body felt things, but they couldn't touch him.

Nicholas barely had to exert any pressure at all to lodge his cock back into Ray's wet hole, a little hitch of his hips and he was in. He sighed his pleasure as he shifted inside Ray's well-lubricated passage, the whole length of him feeling like it was rearranging Ray's insides. And it reached Ray too, turning the uncomfortable fullness into ripe sensuality with the power of Nicholas's need. The wolf pushed into it and Nicholas groaned, speeding his movements inside Ray. He murmured little praises to Ray's arse, his hotness, his wetness, how well he took it.

Ray was hard under him, but it was just a fact, just his cock bouncing with Nicholas's thrusts. Just his balls heavy and full and ready as Nicholas clutched at his legs hard enough to bruise and went for it, ramming into Ray like he wanted to tear him apart, holding him in place with a bruising grip. The orgasm that was building inside him felt as out of Ray's control as the tide, as distant as the moon. The noises of Nicholas's hard dick sliding through his own juices again and again, the slap of skin on skin... It was like a song playing in the background. His whole body; the pain of being split open hard and fast, and the pleasure of Nicholas's cock pressing into his prostate were more like something he was aware of than something he could feel.

Nicholas howled his pleasure as he emptied himself inside Ray's body, the hot liquid spilling down Ray's buttocks as the alpha kept shoving into him. It made Ray finish, too, of course, punching it out of him so fast and sudden it was more surprise than pleasure. His nerves tingled, but his mind couldn't cope; he was too numb for the endorphins to do anything but daze him further.

Nicholas didn't stop once he'd come, just slowed down his thrusts. Ray kept his eyes closed, sparing himself what little he could. And then he felt it: Nicholas's cock was growing, stretching him further. He didn't think, didn't hesitate, just bucked with all his strength, suddenly stricken by a fury so powerful, it didn't matter that Nicholas was stronger and weighing him down. Just like that, the wolf's passivity turned into fierce undiluted hatred and he found the strength to shove him off. He rolled to the side, but he didn't run. He didn't even think of it, just reached for Nicholas's throat and grabbed him hard.

Ray didn't see his own claws, not until they'd pierced the delicate skin. But he didn't open his fist when he saw it, he dug in instead. It was instinct to finish off a fallen threat, and for a moment, with the moon high in the sky, instinct was all Ray was.

He pulled his hand back and watched the blood bloom as if from a distance, so cold to it that he was surprised to see Nicholas reach up to cover the gash, his hands uselessly trying to staunch the torrent of blood pouring out. He scrambled out of reach as understanding reached the alpha's terrified eyes. Nicholas tried to speak, right before he fell on his side, but he had no voice to speak with. Some dark and horrible part of Ray crowed at that.

The wolf howled inside him, the blood had brought the whole scene clearly into the territory of fighting. *Protect the pack*, Ray told it. He didn't imagine the wolf understood words but it'd recognize what Ray was feeling. If there was anything under the numbness of the man watching the half-naked body cool on the ground.

"Ray?"

He looked up at the sound, teeth drawn, and found Gabriel watching him in horror.

"Are you...?" the alpha glanced at the body, then at Ray's destroyed clothes. "Are you okay?"

"The..." Ray tried to say, and his throat was so dry he choked. He swallowed and pushed through it, there was no pain strong enough to keep him from asking, "The babies?"

Gabriel's face fell. "I don't know. I came for you, the others—"

But Ray didn't hear the rest, he'd already shifted and started running back.

Chapter 10

There was blood in the front garden, Ray could smell it even though his own paws were still stained with it. He couldn't tell who it belonged to, not without stopping, and there was no stopping. The same way he couldn't manage to concentrate enough to find the others with his mind.

But they must have heard him approaching because the front door burst open and Sergi and Josh were there. Ray tried to shove between them, but before he had a chance to try and sneak past their legs, they'd tackled him to the ground. They all tangled together, arms, legs, paws and fur pulling uncomfortably. Ray snapped at Josh in warning. *He needed to see them. They had to be okay...*

"Ray," Josh said, shaking him by the scruff of his neck. His grip was unrelenting enough that Ray's wolf whined. "Yes," Josh said. "Listen to me. We are all fine."

Ray whined again, squirming against Sergi's grip on his middle. But Josh refused to budge. "Do you understand what I'm saying? We are all okay. We drove them off. But the kids are still scared, you have to calm down before you go in."

Ray did understand. The words made sense to his human brain even in wolf form, but it didn't matter how much he trusted Josh; it wasn't enough. He whimpered as the wolf got increasingly desperate inside him.

163

"Fuck," Josh said above him, then he raised his voice. "Alec! Bring them out!"

Ray's wolf froze as the sound of little paws on wooden floors reached his ears and Josh moved out of the way to allow him an unrestricted view of Clara running towards him. Jamie was second and then there were all there, nuzzling at him and yipping their joy at being reunited. Ray licked at them, pushing them around to check there wasn't anything wrong with them.

They were okay. He hadn't let them be harmed. He'd done well.

J osh had sat at the foot of the stairs and watched them play. A little while later, Iesu and Alec had come outside and given them all fresh water and some less than fresh meat—nobody had planned for it to be eaten raw—so by the time it occurred to Ray to be worried about his alphas, he already knew they were all okay.

But then it was bedtime and he'd reluctantly led the pups back inside and into the bathroom to get them cleaned up for bed. He didn't want to leave them, but when Iesu and Sergi had come in to give them their bath, he'd realised that if he wanted to help, he'd need to change back.

He'd settled outside the bathroom door to rest instead, eyes closed but ears open to any disturbances. He'd heard Gabriel way before he spoke, ignoring Ray's pretence of sleep.

"Don't you want a shower?" his cousin asked.

Ray had lifted his head from his paws to give him an unimpressed look. He wanted to be clean about as much as he wanted the day to have never happened, but the idea of shifting back and letting anybody see the state his body was in made him even more nauseous than Nicholas's scent still clinging to him.

"You don't need to shift," Gabriel offered with rare insight. "I can help," he added, then lowered his eyes. "Or I can get Josh."

He glanced up at Ray. "Just... lift your right paw or something and I will get him for you."

Ray hesitated. But Gabriel had seen it. Gabriel had to know. Anybody with a nose had to know, but it wouldn't hurt to cling to the illusion for a little longer that it was only Gabriel. He stood and padded past his cousin, pausing only for a moment to signal he expected to be followed.

Gabriel rushed ahead to the other bathroom to heat up the water for him, then closed the door behind them. Ray jumped into the tub easily—his body was almost completely healed by now. But Gabriel was still gentle with him, like maybe he knew the cuts might be closed but Ray remembered getting them. He got Ray wet and then dropped half a bottle of flowery smelling baby shampoo on him. It made Ray sneeze, but anything was better than the way he'd smelt for the last hours, and after Gabriel rinsed it off him, carefully carding his fingers through Ray's fur, he didn't mind the mild scent much.

He made Gabriel squawk when he shook off the excess water, but his cousin still patiently patted him dry afterwards. His silence was as precious to Ray as his attention to detail. It was easier not to think as a wolf, but only if nobody tried to bring the human parts of his brain to the forefront.

Ray went right back to the main bathroom afterwards, poking his head in to find that the pups had got the better of Iesu and Sergi and made a total mess of the place. They were all still shifted, he noticed. Maybe they'd forgotten they didn't have to follow Ray's lead.

Or maybe they felt safer that way. Ray growled a warning when Clara tried to sneak past him, and she immediately froze in place, looking up at him with big pleading eyes. He indicated they should all follow him and ignored Sergi's groans about them trailing water all over the corridor.

The bedspread got a little wet when they all curled on top of it, but with his pups warm and safe around him, Ray couldn't have cared less if they had flooded half the house.

Josh woke him up the next morning with a hand on his neck, digging deep behind his ears in a way he found irresistible.

"Alec's gone to get you more meat," he whispered from where he was leaning against Ray's side. Ray had thought he'd sleep with an eye open, but he'd dropped like a rock once he'd felt safe enough. Josh had sneaked in without alarming him at all.

Of course, it could have been that the wolf knew its mate, even unconscious.

Just like Josh knew Ray wasn't ready to shift back and talk. Gabriel must have told them that Nicholas was dead, maybe even that Ray had done it, but... If they hadn't guessed the rest, Ray would have to speak of it.

So they got him more fresh meat and, all in all, it was a lot easier to let the pups run in the garden with Ray than make sure they didn't crawl away or transform out of their nappies and leave a surprise for them to step on. Since they had the time, Ray decided to try and teach them to catch a squirrel. It was not a great success, but it was still pretty entertaining.

After work that afternoon, Iesu had come and joined them, tail wagging happily like he was a pup himself. And of course, it wasn't hard to get Sergi when he tried to walk in after work. Even better, it turned out he'd brought them fresh lamb, or as fresh as the butcher's ever was. They could have hunted, but they knew Ray preferred bigger animals to rabbits.

Neither they nor Josh, who didn't shift and instead curled up with little Michael in his lap and watched them again, tried to talk about anything serious.

But deep down, Ray knew it couldn't last.

He couldn't hide forever.

He gave himself that night, one more night of warmth and safety, and he'd change back and face the music. Maybe they suspected he needed the support, or maybe they had simply been worried sick and only stayed away for his sake because that night Josh had walked into Ray's bedroom to ask for permission to join him.

In response, Ray had jumped onto the floor and dragged the covers down with his teeth. There was no way six adults and five pups could fit into one bed, not even one as large as his.

Josh had laughed and helped him pull—Ray did miss having hands—and called for the others to come over. Alec had clearly been waiting right behind Josh. Ray was no fool; if Alec had caught even a hint of what had happened, he'd want to examine Ray to reassure himself he was okay. Soon Sergi and Iesu had followed with extra pillows. Gabriel had been last, still looking oddly subdued, and he'd waited by the doorway until Ray had looked up from where little Maria was licking his ear and met his eyes.

While the others made an effort to get close to Ray, even if only to rub their sides together for a moment, Gabriel stayed away in the edges of the circle. Ray was almost sorry for him, but that was only because he was too tired to be angry.

Ray knew his own mistake had been grave, and he didn't think he'd ever forgive himself for it, not even after the price he'd paid. But he still couldn't forgive his alpha for leaving their children behind when he knew they were in danger. Not even to look for Ray. Maybe especially not to look for Ray, who didn't deserve it. Gabriel should have known Ray would have never wanted it, not truly.

Chapter 11

He hadn't given himself any time to hesitate. The moment he'd opened his eyes, he'd disentangled himself from the bodies on the floor and squirmed his way to the other side of the room. Then he'd shifted.

It was only when he was on all fours on the floor, legs and arms trembling in shock, that he'd realised he was completely naked. He was used to being naked. Werewolves didn't grow up with the hang-ups humans had about their bodies; it was simply too impractical to manage when you had to undress to shift and you'd shift back into human form without any clothing.

But as he rolled to his feet and scanned the dresser for a shirt, a towel, *anything*, Ray realised that he did care. He found a shirt and shoved his arms into it so roughly the seams tore a little, and then shoved his legs into a pair of jeans that had got stuck behind the dresser without worrying about underwear.

And only then had he thought to check on the alphas.

They were all still asleep. Only Sasha was looking at him, luminous dark eyes curious and wide. After a moment, in the way the pups tended to do around him, she decided she'd rather have skin than fur. She beamed up at him as if expecting him to be proud of her achievement, and Ray's knees went weak.

The thing was... he was proud. He crouched and picked her up, holding her in his arms like she was still the fragile creature he'd given birth to. To him, she would always be. She clung back, shoving her face into his chest in a way that was not completely in line with her human features.

He breathed her in. Just let her scent and her warmth and her heartbeat, steady and sure, calm down his own racing pulse.

It was going to be okay. She was okay. They were all okay and that meant whatever had happened hadn't broken them. It had been scary, and it'd hurt, and he was going to have nightmares for the rest of his life. But it was going to be okay.

He could survive anything, if he had them.

Alec had woken first—he claimed getting up at insane times to get to university while still living close enough to his pack had forever messed up his circadian rhythms—and because he was Alec, he hadn't been able to disguise his relief.

Ray had offered him a smile from where he was holding Maria to his chest. He'd been trying to wean them out—anxious to let his body go back to normal while he still had time and desperate for a way to regain at least some of his independence—but now he only wanted to feel them close. Alec knew but didn't say anything.

"Morning," Alec said a little timidly, then turned on the kitchen radio and started making breakfast while humming along. He couldn't bear the silence, so he was giving Ray the space he needed in the only way he could.

Ray was grateful, he was okay with the babies, who couldn't talk, much less understand, but he didn't know if he could bear a conversation with one of his mates. Everything that had happened seemed to be about to burst out of him: the pain, and the guilt, and the deep abiding fear. He didn't even know what had happened with Nicholas's gang, he realised as he gazed right through the back door of the kitchen.

The sound of his name startled him into awareness. Iesu was standing in front of him, looking less cheery than Ray had ever seen him.

"You were a million miles away," his alpha said. Ray nodded. "Give her here, your food is getting cold."

And it was true; there was a full English breakfast still smoking on a plate in front of him. He shook his head and gave Maria to Iesu without a word. She complained loudly about the interrupted feeding, but Alec was quick to distract her with a bib. And the food was hot, greasy and good. After a few bites, it seemed to revive something in him—at least the wolf's appetite was intact.

The others had filtered in soon after, probably attracted by the irresistible scent of bacon. But Ray hadn't looked up from his plate and they hadn't tried to engage him.

It reminded him of old times, but it was for the best. He was capable of speech again, but the words didn't seem to be in his head to be said. And what could they say that wasn't all wrong? They had to know. They couldn't have failed to smell it on him, even if Gabriel hadn't told them and... Ray shuddered in place and dug his nails into the skin of his thigh under the table to force his thoughts from the memories of pain much more intense than a scratch.

Iesu froze next to him, but he let it go without comment. And Ray was grateful for that, even if he would have been even more grateful for something that took the thoughts away.

He didn't know what; it was just that it felt like it had to exist. If he had to keep tiptoeing inside his own head, he was going to fall into a black hole and never come out again.

He'd been expecting one of the alphas. But it was his sister who came to look for him once he retired to his bedroom alone. She and the other betas had been giving Ray and the alphas space since... since Ray's return. And it wasn't like they'd have been able to talk when he'd been a wolf anyway.

He didn't want to talk now, but he'd been so braced for what he knew was coming with his mates that talking to Marisa seemed like nothing in comparison.

"Do you want me to go?" she asked, still in the doorway.

"What?" Ray asked, confused, and stepped back, leaving the path clear for her to walk in.

She stepped in and let him, already explaining in a high, thready voice, "I... I can't ever apologize enough, Ray." She was on the verge of tears. "But I can go, if—"

"Apologize?"

"I *let him take you*," his sister gritted out, full of pain and frustration.

"What are you talking about?" Ray asked, sitting down on the bed. "You didn't know, and you couldn't have left the pups anyway."

"I had my phone, Ray," she explained in a strangled voice. "But I was too stupid to notice you had gone to make tea and hadn't come back for *twenty* minutes."

He stood up and stepped up to her, taking her by the shoulders. "*I* let them in, and I left you with them. If anybody should apologize..."

That seemed to break her determination. She fell forward, clutching at him and started to cry like a dam inside her had broken. Ray held her smaller body to his. She'd always been such a good kid; obedient and helpful even when she'd been little.

"I'm sorry," she said again in between sobs. "I came to help... I swear."

"I know you did, sweetheart," he assured her, not letting her move away from him. "And you have."

"How could he...?" she started to ask before her voice gave out.

Ray had to take a moment before he could calm down enough to answer. "I don't know."

Something in his voice must have given away his despair because Marisa pushed him away enough to look him in the face. "Oh, no," she murmured, and Ray realised she hadn't known.

Of course not, she hadn't seen him that night. She could barely imagine an alpha *kidnapping* an omega, let alone...

He stiffened, but Marisa dug her hands into his clothes. He turned his face from hers, feeling himself flush. His skin was crawling—intense, stomach-turning revulsion making him shudder as he remembered Nicholas on top him—and it was all he could do to stay still.

It was only the fact that it was his little sister that kept him locked in place—there was possibly no one else in the world he'd have trusted to touch him in that moment. And he couldn't bear to hurt her anymore—he'd promised his mum he'd keep her safe. So he let her hold onto him even if it took digging his nails into his own hands to keep from jumping away like she was on fire.

"I didn't... *Ray.*" She was crying harder now, but Ray couldn't make himself hold her back. He stood there and let her cry on his shirt—as much as he could manage without falling to pieces.

There was nothing wrong with her, of course—it was he who was tainted.

It seemed like a long time, but eventually, she calmed down enough to pull back. Ray kept his gaze on the one picture he'd hung in the room. He knew it was a portrait of the pups sleeping in a pile, but in that moment, it could have been anything.

"Do you want to be alone?" she asked in a thick voice.

Ray nodded, feeling strangely calm—the frantic desperation had subsided in the minutes he'd stood there. He couldn't meet her eyes—he wasn't sure he'd ever be able to again—but he no longer wanted to wrench himself away.

In a way, it was like he already had.

When he thought of her again, he realised she'd already gone.

He hadn't wanted her to know. He hadn't wanted anybody to know. He knew it was impossible that they didn't, even if Gabriel hadn't seen him; he had hardly been in the state of mind to jump into the lake on his way over to the house. But it was worse that it was Marisa.

Or maybe it was the fact that she'd acknowledged it. She hadn't said the word, but that didn't seem to matter because talking about it seemed to wrench something free in Ray's mind. He woke in the middle of the night, tangled in his own bedclothes—throat hoarse and t-shirt wet with sweat despite the cold—and flinched when he found Gabriel standing a few feet away. He'd clearly come to check on him.

"You were having a nightmare," his alpha explained, hesitantly.

Ray looked away from him and gestured for him to go away. Gabriel either misunderstood or ignored it because he sat at the foot of the bed instead—far enough away that he wasn't even close to the area where Ray's feet would have been if he hadn't been curled up in a ball. "Want a glass of milk? We could watch the ending of that documentary."

Ray hesitated. His whole body ached—probably from fighting against himself all night—and the shadow of the nightmare still lingered in his mind. Except it wasn't a nightmare; it was a memory.

He could hardly erase the past. "I want a latte," he told Gabriel, and his alpha didn't argue that coffee would keep Ray up the rest of the night, just got to his feet.

"Coming right up."

When Ray joined him in the TV room, the drink was on the side table and the TV was on to the news channel. Ray had never met a werewolf who cared as much about the petty messes of humans as Gabriel did. He glanced at the screen; there was a war somewhere and the deaths numbered beyond the number of werewolves in the whole world.

"Sorry," Gabriel said, and clicked through until he found the documentary about lions they'd been watching earlier. It still had a lot of humans in it, what with the way they'd fucked up half the lions' territory, but at least they only came up sometimes.

Ray had always thought wild animals made a lot more sense than people. They could be brutal, but they weren't cruel.

After a while, Gabriel offered him a blanket and Ray took it, then sat back down a little closer. Gabriel tilted his body towards him without looking away from the lion cubs play-fighting onscreen. He didn't try to touch Ray, but the offer was clear.

At some point, Ray must have fallen asleep because the sun streaming through the living room window woke him up. He didn't know if Gabriel had slept too, but he was in the kitchen already and there was fresh coffee.

Ray hadn't liked him this much since he'd been twelve and Gabriel had taken them all the zoo, but he could have almost thanked him for his silence now. Except that would have defeated the point, of course.

Maybe he'd thank him one day; now he needed it too much to ruin it.

Epilogue

"**R**ay, are you okay?" Iesu asked with a frown.

Ray made a face, swallowing against the need to retch. "Is that broccoli *off*?" he demanded.

Iesu sniffed, shaking his head already. "No. I mean, it's broccoli so it's pretty smelly, but it smells fine to me."

Ray shrugged. "I guess it's trauma from that time..."

"That was pretty epic," Iesu admitted and placed a lid on the boiling pot. "Better?"

Ray nodded even though his stomach still felt weirdly unsettled. "Aren't there other healthy vegetables that we could be having?"

He knew he was whining, but he'd slept badly. He hadn't had a nightmare for once, and Jamie had gone to sleep with a baby bottle. But then his son had woken before sunrise, and Ray hadn't been able to get back to sleep himself afterwards. He felt moody and off. It was only noon and his body was convinced it was mid-afternoon.

"I'll get you a plate of stew, you can eat in your room," Iesu offered. Marisa had decided they needed to optimize their use of meat by mixing it with vegetables. So far Ray hadn't minded not having steaks or racks every night, and rabbit meat was good for stews, but he drew the line at broccoli. If things hadn't been so fragile between his sister and him, he might have even told her. But even less than smelly food, he couldn't bear her pity.

"Thanks," he told Iesu. "I wanted to look up some designs for bunk beds anyway."

At the rate the babies were growing, they'd need their own beds soon and even if the betas moved out into the new wing soon—assuming someone got enough money to pay for the plumbing to get done—that meant bunk beds. Ray didn't even want to think of the cost of raising five children, and a part of him could never forget this was only the beginning.

Iesu bowed theatrically. "At your service."

Ray forced a smile, already preoccupied with his thoughts.

Gabriel couldn't have been the only one who heard him wake up screaming. They didn't have any special soundproofing. The babies had been sleeping with Alec or Josh more often than not because they had the rooms farthest from Ray's. Ray had woken them up with his dreaming exactly once and he'd felt so guilty, he'd nearly cried himself. They hadn't spoken about it to him, but Ray knew they must have agreed to let Gabriel handle it.

It didn't bother Ray, except that a part of him expected that role to fall to Josh. Josh, who'd told him he loved him right before Nicholas had taken him and now... But what was Josh supposed to say?

Ray didn't want to spend time with him alone anyway, not really. If having Josh see him as an omega had been mortifying, having Josh know what he'd let Nicholas do to him was...

revolting. No amount of showering could get rid of the feeling of wanting to peel off his own skin that overtook him anytime he remembered.

All the alphas were avoiding all touch but the most casual of taps, and that couldn't be a coincidence either. Ray didn't want to need the special treatment, but he was too afraid of finding out if touch really would make him feel as bad as the memory of it did. He knew he'd need to be able to handle it soon enough; they might have missed a full moon, but that was bound to make them need it more the next time the Goddess rose in the sky. Or sooner.

But maybe heat would take care of Ray's reluctance. He could only hope that he could afford the time and distance he was too weak not to take. He hoped Josh wasn't angry at him—not that he'd been anything but doting, but Josh would probably do that no matter what. He wouldn't show it, not even if he was disgusted with Ray.

With Marisa and the other betas taking over some of the housework and childcare, all the alphas that had the chance were working overtime. They'd always needed the money, and now they were finalising the construction of the beta wing of the house, and they'd also decided they needed to plant some sensors on the outer edges of the territory. It shouldn't have been just Ray who could tell if a stranger walked in on them.

It was the right thing to do, for the pups, for them... but it made Ray realise how badly he'd failed. Being First Omega of a pack was being its last line of defence, and Ray had taken it lightly and risked all their lives. He was lucky he'd been the only one the alphas had hurt. If anybody else had...

He didn't know if his instincts—the same that pushed him to do things that felt so contrary to his own desires—were broken, or if he was just a naïve idiot. Not that it mattered; he had proof that he couldn't trust himself to do the job on his own. There was no way he'd risk it again.

It was the same reason he could no longer delay choosing a first alpha. A first omega had powers no other wolf in their pack did, but they weren't meant to keep that power to themselves. He was supposed to choose an alpha among his mates to share his power. He'd bite the alpha he chose to give him the power to read Ray's emotions in turn.

But he was scared. Because biting an alpha himself would mean completing the circle of magic between them, it would mean a mutual bond that would be considerably stronger than what he already shared with each of them. And all Ray wanted was to hide all the broken pieces of his mind and heart that he had managed to hold on to. He didn't want to share his pain; he wanted it to go away.

A mutual bond had been customary between all mated alphas and omegas once. But nowadays most people found it too overwhelming to be fully bonded when they had to separate for work and travel, so only first omegas were truly expected to do it—and even they had some leeway. Nobody had told Ray it was necessary, but now he didn't need to be told. He'd felt completely untethered from his pack when Nicholas had taken him, lost because he hadn't tied anybody to him, and his bond with the alphas wasn't strong enough to communicate his distress.

Nobody had brought it up before, but Ray had known that if he were to choose, he was expected to choose Gabriel. His cousin had taken over leadership of the pack so naturally that even though he made Ray uncomfortable, he hadn't thought to object to what he knew was coming.

For a few days after they'd talked about their shared past, Ray had hoped they'd be able to find a balance. But that was over now. Gabriel had to know it as well as Ray. Ray had paid the price already, now it was Gabriel's turn. Anytime before, Ray would have been relieved to have a reason to turn his overbearing alpha away and choose with his heart instead. But not now.

He couldn't even imagine how to tell Josh. He was still angry at Gabriel, but at least he knew where they stood. He knew Gabriel would support him, but not ask him for anything he couldn't give. Except Gabriel had failed, too. He'd failed Ray, and the pups, and the pack. He wasn't the right choice. Josh was.

Josh was kind; he wouldn't bring up what Nicholas had done, or make a fuss about the fact that Ray hadn't stopped it. He'd be kind, loyal, and he'd become Ray's First Alpha to keep their pack safe.

He hadn't made Ray any promises—a confession was not any more binding than feelings by themselves. If Ray didn't ask, he wouldn't have to take it back. Ray had been determined to keep things from getting too complicated between them anyway—the risk of loving Josh openly, of admitting his preference, wasn't worth his pack's safety. And having said it, it'd be easier to move on from it. Josh wasn't perfect and being Ray's First Alpha would indubitably lead them to clashing before long. It would be easy to get angry at him, to resent the power Ray had given him because he needed his steering hand more than he needed his own freedom.

Ray didn't doubt Josh would keep him safe, but it was hard to sincerely love someone with so much power over you. It was for the best, too; if the price of their safety was the romance they shouldn't have had anyway.

But Josh was away at work, Irina was looking after the kids, and Ray was so tired still. Nicholas was dead and the other alphas had been taken back to their birth packs to be dealt with. It was over. Except maybe in Ray's head. He didn't know how to stop wondering what he could have done better, or how he'd live with what he had done. But he had a little peace now, a few more hours of silence before he faced yet another great change in his life. Maybe he didn't deserve it, maybe it was just more proof of his weakness but he would take it.

Breaking his own heart could wait one more day.

[End book II]

If you enjoyed this story, you can go straight to book 3, **Protectors of the Pack**. Or join my mailing list[1] and you will get the alternative chapter to this book (a little heavier on the kink, if you will :p).

---

1. https://readerlinks.com/l/1705735

Protectors of the Pack - Excerpt

Alec had been too busy with university to hit the clubs all that often, but it was almost full moon and he'd needed to get out of his flat. Away from his books, and his laptop, and his bloody oblivious flatmates walking around shirtless—and sometimes a lot more than that, if they'd run out of clean clothes.

It seemed so unfair that he had to deal with his body on top of everything else. It'd never bothered him much growing up; he'd always been small for his age, but that had only been a problem in his *mind*. And the minds of everyone else in his pack, of course: he had a perfect werewolf immune system, the speed and agility... but with his size and personality, he'd got teased a lot. It never got to the point where it could be called bullying, although Alec thought that was mostly because at school all the wolves had each other's backs. It didn't matter which kind of wolf Alec would grow up to be, next to a human, he was pack and pack always came first.

And at home, he'd made it as easy for them to leave him alone. He'd hung out with the other pack children only until he'd started secondary school, and then he'd clung to homework as a reason to stay home and away from them. His mum had still made him go to family meetings and the occasional dinner with friends—hers and his dad's—and she liked to pretend he had his own relationships with their children. But it wasn't too bad.

He was lonely, but it was better than being afraid of running his mouth all the time. If he was alone, he didn't have to wonder whether he should say things or not, or whether his silence was disturbing in itself. Or whether other boys could tell his eyes wandered towards them instead of their sisters when they all went to the lake.

His parents were both sociable, likeable people and they kept asking Alec to watch movies with them, or share what he'd learned in school—even if all Alec managed was a few disconnected phrases. Not that he was uncomfortable around them, it was more like he was uncomfortable being himself. He admired his father's easy confidence and his mother effortless charm, and both seemed so completely out of his reach that his poor attempts to imitate them were torture.

Alec did not do well with failure. He was clever, but it was that more than anything else that ensured his academic success. If you couldn't bear to fail, you did not skip on that extra revision session. After a while, it was easy—he developed his own systems and shortcuts, and his brain was used to the exercise. He couldn't really stop studying—the fear of failure was too intense—but he allowed himself to read more in-depth books about the topic instead of compulsively re-reading his notes and textbooks. He loved it, he really did. But more than that: he needed it. He needed to know there was something in the world he could control, something at which he could always succeed.

His parents never talked about it, but Alec was too smart not to know that they had no hopes he'd be an alpha. He wasn't sure if they preferred beta or omega. Not that omega was likely. Alec was okay with remaining a beta, if he was a beta, he wouldn't be forced to get a mate. A woman. He wouldn't be forced to mate a woman. He would have liked a man, of course, but he could barely bring himself to talk to people his age at dinner when his parents dragged him over to their friends—dating was a mirage.

And if he was an omega... Well, that would explain why he liked boys. It would make it okay, male omegas were mated to male alphas, after all. Nobody said it was okay, of course. Werewolves as a whole followed human culture all too gladly—including their media and art, and despite the fact that so many of the things humans revered were completely against the survival of wolf packs. The way they used the land alone... At least liking boys had got easier over time, but it'd never got to be *easy*. And all boys were expected to want to be alphas, even if they had no chance in hell of ever becoming one, and as alphas, to want to procreate above all things. If the occasion arose, exceptions were made for omega males on both the parts of the alphas and the omega.

But omega males were too rare to do much more than blip the radar... After taking a couple of statistics courses and finding out the numbers of omegas in some other packs, Alec had decided the chances of him being an omega were low, as in less likely than winning the lottery. But he could be a beta. And he could be gay. Some betas could have kids, and some couldn't. So long as they were helping the pack, nobody much minded if they were single.

And at uni, in a city full of humans who didn't even know Alec was too short and too slight for a grown wolf, it was almost like being normal. Just human, no wolf in sight. Alphas and omegas had trouble controlling their instincts, but other than the need to run and hunt during the full moon, betas weren't really affected.

In the human world, Alec had to admit he had it pretty great: nobody had the strength to beat him up if he propositioned the wrong person in a club, and even though he spent more time in the library than anywhere else, he still had the kind of body they put on ads. He hated dancing with a passion, of course, even though he rationally knew nobody would laugh at him if he fumbled the steps. In gay clubs, there *weren't* even steps beyond grinding. But he didn't need to dance, just put on tight clothes, get a drink and lean against a handy surface until someone caught his eye, or came over. It'd have been an utter failure to pick up girls, but it worked wonders on guys because it made it clear that he was both available and willing to hook up without too much fuss.

Most of the time, they didn't even need to talk. It was enough with hands and mouths and moans. He didn't bring them back to his place—not because of his flatmates, but because his sense of smell meant he'd have smelled them all over his room for weeks—but there was a lot you could do in a toilet stall, or the corner of a darkened room. He didn't go back to theirs that often either, he didn't want to have to navigate the small talk during the trip. He had fun, and he was dealing fine with his instincts, really, except when it got close to the moon like this and it wasn't *enough*.

He thought about going running in the park instead, give his wolf free reign. But the full moon was in two days and he didn't trust his wolf. He didn't really trust himself either, not around a vulnerable human body, but if he kept it quick...

Alec walked into a club he knew pretty well and discovered between seconds that it was completely changed. Nobody else would notice, of course, but the scent of a wolf hung heavy and thick over the whole place. An alpha, which maybe explained why he'd felt the need to walk the perimeter of the room. Alec stood there, too stunned by the way his two lives had collided to do much at all, until a heavy hand had closed on his upper arm. He'd turned his head at once and met blue eyes like ice. The club was loud and busy enough he hadn't heard anyone approaching.

The alpha was still in the room, and he wasn't happy to see him.

"Come with me," he'd said, and it felt like a compulsion. Alec had followed him out in a daze.

It didn't occur to him that it could be dangerous to go somewhere alone with *this* stranger until they were outside and he saw the man's face. His eyes were even bluer under the nightlights and his blond hair shone actual gold in parts.

"Oh, it's you." He regretted the words as soon as he saw the confusion on the alpha's face.

"Do we know each other?"

Alec shrugged and the alpha let go of his arm. It shouldn't have been a relief, it wasn't like he couldn't tell how fast Alec's heart was going anyway. Or like Alec could outrun an alpha so much bigger than him. "Not really, but I've seen you around Havant territory."

"You are pack," the alpha said, sounding shocked. Then he inhaled, frowning when he got a whiff of Alec's scent. "How long since you haven't been back?"

Alec shrugged. "I'm studying medicine, it gets crazy."

And then the hand returned, this time to the bare skin of his wrist. He jerked with both the feeling of skin on skin and surprise. The alpha was burning up, and when Alec met his eyes, he smiled. "Moon crazy, I think you mean. You're like a furnace."

Alec stared. "I'm sorry if—"

"Oh, don't," the stranger said, pulling him a step closer with easy strength. He'd been close before, now his shoes were touching Alec's. He shivered. "What's your name?"

"Alec."

"Gabriel Gosden." The alpha's smile was sharp. Gosden, like the pack's First Alpha. Alec had recognised his face—he was antisocial, not blind—but he hadn't known he was talking to a member of his own Pack's inner circle.

"Oh, like..."

"My uncle," Gabriel said, then glanced down to where his thumb was rubbing circles against the inside of Alec's wrist. Alec's whole body felt overheated and overstimulated—like he'd been under the alpha's hands for hours, not minutes.

He'd thought the alpha was angry at him for walking into a club he considered his. But Gabriel hadn't walked the perimeter for fun or paranoia, he'd caught *Alec's* scent and wanted to replace it with his own. Maybe he hadn't been able to tell Alec was only a beta—not if he'd missed that they were from the same pack.

And now that he'd found out... Gabriel was an alpha in a human gay bar, close to the full moon. If it was dangerous for Alec to be there; for an alpha... "Do you want to run?" he asked in his steadiest voice. His body didn't betray him. Not beyond the flush he could feel on his cheeks anyway.

Gabriel's lips parted and it was all Alec could do to keep himself from flinching at the incredulity on his face. But he did lower his gaze, trying to save himself some of the humiliation, and Gabriel used the distraction to yank him even closer. And then he was sliding his other hand up Alec's neck, tangling his fingers in his hair, and forcing his face up into a kiss.

Gabriel's mouth was as hot as the rest of him, and he didn't go easy on him—like Alec had to do with humans. He just pushed his tongue into Alec's mouth until Alec opened up and started sucking on it. He tasted good, like beer and something sweeter, and his leather jacket was soft under Alec's hands, even if he was afraid of ripping it with his claws. He bit on Alec's lips—only soft enough not to draw blood—and pushed their torsos together. His cock hard pressed against Alec's belly and his bent knee against his erection.

He was aware of what was happening, but it was like he couldn't make himself *believe* it.

Because he'd thought about it. He'd wanted another wolf under him, and it had always seemed so completely impossible... He shoved Gabriel hard against a wall, just because he could. Because it wouldn't hurt him, because it would be *real*. Gabriel's back thudded against the side of the alley like he was made of rock himself and he let out a low growl in his throat. Alec's heartbeat spiked in alarm. Of course a beta couldn't push an *alpha*. But he didn't have time to get really afraid, because all the other man did was dig his claws into Alec's clothes and reverse their positions, slamming him against the wall instead. It hurt a little, but it rattled Alec even more because being pinned like that sent a rush of arousal through him like fire spreading down a dry forest in summer. He whimpered, confused and so hard it was painful.

"Watch it," Gabriel warned, but it wasn't that upsetting when he went right back to kissing Alec. The anger in how he forced Alec's mouth to open for him was making his dick throb too much for his brain to mind. If he'd been really offended, he wouldn't have stayed, after all. "God, I needed this," he mumbled as he nibbled at Alec's throat.

Nobody was supposed to touch him there at all and Gabriel hadn't even *asked,* but Alec let his head roll to the side to give him room. Almost as if to reward him, Gabriel's hand sneaked down their bodies and undid their zips. They groaned together in relief, and Gabriel snorted, like he thought it was too much like porn. But Alec didn't care, not when Gabriel's hand pushed into his underwear—big and powerful and clenching tight against his dick—and pulled him out. He whimpered and tried to help, but Gabriel elbowed his hand away. "Just stay," he said. And Alec did.

It was good he did, too. Thirty seconds later Gabriel had pushed their cocks against each other and was jerking them off, slow because there wasn't enough lubrication and it almost hurt. But also *so good,* so absolutely *real.* Nothing like doing it to himself, and not even like doing it with a human. They were always so fucking careful with his junk—maybe because they couldn't have taken the kind of heat, the kind of pressure, the kind of... They couldn't have taken what Alec wanted. What he needed.

But he didn't need to tell Gabriel he wouldn't break. Gabriel just *knew*. He keened high in his throat, unable to help himself, and clutched at Gabriel's thick arms as the alpha kept jerking them off, their hips so close together they were probably going to come all over each other's clothes.

And then Gabriel yanked Alec's hand between their bodies and made him cup it around the tips. "Now," he growled, and it was like he had a direct line to Alec's cock because that was all it took to get him to come, erupting like a volcano, muscles locking against the wave of pleasure. Gabriel tightened his grip on both of them, spreading Alec's come over both their cocks and groaning at the added slickness until Alec was about to beg him to stop. And then he buried his face into Alec's neck and started coming himself, almost shaking apart in Alec's arms.

They stood there, panting, as their skin cooled and their heartbeats slowed. If he hadn't been caged against the wall by Gabriel's body, Alec would have probably tried to shuffle away, or at least clean himself; but he couldn't quite bring himself to push the man away for practical matters. He'd never had sex like that before, even if he'd only been a shared handjob, and it was dawning on him that he wasn't likely to get another chance.

Finally, Gabriel straightened. Alec glanced down between them to assess the state of their clothes and discovered that Gabriel was still holding his hand cupped around their cockheads. It was like his body had been too overwhelmed to register the stickiness but he'd caught a fair amount of both their come. The rest Gabriel must have aimed to the side; there was a mess at their feet.

"Huh, are you sure you are a beta?" The alpha had teased him. Alphas were supposed to produce considerably more ejaculate, but it hadn't occurred to Alec that Gabriel maybe had a point despite all the evidence. Looking back, he wasn't sure if it was that people had got it into his head that he couldn't be an alpha, or that he just had never wanted it to be true.

Alec had grimaced and shaken his hand to the side, then turned to clean the rest against the wall. But Gabriel had easily caught his wrist again and pulled his hand towards himself. He'd met Alec's eyes as he licked their mingled come off Alec's fingers like it was a delicacy. Alec had watched him swallow with as much attention as he might have paid someone performing surgery on his own heart, and Gabriel did it again. He'd slowly cleaned Alec's hand, for all the world looking absolutely delighted to be swallowing their spunk.

"Now we could go running," Gabriel had decided, letting go of Alec. "I'm fairly sure I won't eat any lost puppies."

If you enjoyed this story, check out my website (**www.njlysk.com**) or more. I'd also *love* a review! Reviews let other readers know what they are getting into and help the book get to the right people, plus it's nice to hear what you thought so I know what works and doesn't!

Other Books by N.J. Lysk

N.J.LYSK'S BOOKSHOP
WWW.NJLYSK.COM/SHOP

The Stars of the Pack:

1) **Omega for the Pack** – When Ray presents as an omega instead of an alpha, his life changes forever. As a male omega, he's expected to mate with a select group of alphas and start a pack of his own. **A/B/O, M/M/M/M/M/M, M/M, mpreg, dubcon.** *Also in German, French, Italian & Portuguese.*

1.1) Simpler than Most *(an interlude)* – Sergi has stopped lying to himself: he's had a crush on a guy for a while. But it turns out telling yourself the truth is just the first step of a long journey. *Also in Spanish, German, Italian & French bilingual editions.*

2) **Alpha for the Pack** – Ray wasn't ready to become an omega, but he's come to accept his fate... until it seems the pack might need even more of him than he can give.

3) **Protectors of the Pack** – Alec and Gabriel are Ray's alphas first and foremost and nothing to each other. But three years ago... things were very different.

4) **Beloved of the Pack** – An omega is essential to his pack. But an omega is just a man. And a man needs to be loved. *Can you share your body and not share your heart?*

5) **Betas Aside** – Marisa never hesitated to go to her brother's aid—even when he has what she wants most in the world and can never have. But maybe where there's love, there is a way.

1) **Runt of the Litter** – An older omega who is ready to change the world, a young alpha who doesn't believe in his own potential; a love that's stronger than distance, age or inclination. **A/B/O. M/M. Age gap. Long-distance.**

2) **Paper Kisses** – Abel's not the kind of alpha to make a fuss when his omega ex gets together with someone else, but he's still lonely enough to seek out their kid's teacher to complain about wasting time to celebrate Valentine's day. He doesn't expect to find a lot more than paper hearts. **M/M. Age gap. Human/werewolf. Sweet.**

Rules to Break:

- **Not Destiny** – Thomas and Uriel were never meant to be together. If they choose each other anyway, can they beat the odds? **An Alpha/Beta romance.**
- **Cracking Ice series (7 episodes)** – Hockey means everything to them both... Until they meet each other. **An Alpha/Omega hockey romance.**
- **A Unique Perspective** (*Coming soon*) – Yadriel doesn't look like an omega, but to the eyes of a very interested beta photographer, maybe there is a lot more to him than his size. **A beta/omega BDSM romance.**

Standalones:

- **A Light in Winter** – Alone and trapped by a dangerous arctic storm, two young men have no choice but to confront their feelings for each other. **A/B/O. Cousins. Werewolves. Isolation.**
- **The Omega Sacrifice** - *Fate deals the cards, but you can still play your hand.* When a young omega is sent away to marry a strange alpha, he has no choice but to face who he is. **An arranged marriage omegaverse romance.**
- **A Bond Unbroken** – When Lia presents as an omega, her best friend offers her anything she needs. But Lia's been in love with Amira for years and whatever her wolf wants, her heart cannot take what's not freely given. **Best friends to lovers. F/F. A/B/O.** *Also in Spanish, German, Italian & French.*
- **Truth Unveiled:** When Kala comes out at work to spite her biphobic coworker, she ends up in need of a fake date for the Christmas party. Her best friend immediately offers to help, but for how long can they handle the pretence? **F/F. Shifters, not A/B/O. A best friends fake dating novella.**
- **Omega Under The Moon** – School is over and Cole is ready to take a break before adult life starts, but

when a camping trip with his two best mates turns into something much wilder, it'll change his life forever. **A/B/O. M/M/M.** *Also in French, German & Italian.*

- **Omega On A Mission** - omegas are carers, not fighters, and Gabi is happy looking after his alpha. But when he comes across an animal in danger, his protective instincts flare up, and nobody wants to get in the way of an omega on a mission. **A/B/O.**

Intertwined Fates:

- **Not to be Borne** – When his twin brother presents as an omega, Michuá feels like the world is ending. In a way, becoming an omega himself seems like the only way to stay together… But Zybyn's new alpha wants a lot more than they have bargained for and in a journey towards a strange land, there is nothing to stop him from taking it. **Non-con, abuse, twincest, HEA.**
- **His, Truly** – When Shane unexpectedly presents as an omega during the full moon, his twin brother steps in to protect him from the alphas who'd claim him… But Tim is also an alpha. **A/B/O. M/M. Twincest.** *Also in French & German.*
- **The Realm of the Impossible** – The Queen is dead and Lorax is ready to take his rightful place when an intimate betrayal leaves him with no choice but to surrender his throne or lose his only remaining family. At this unbearable crossroad, Lorax can watch the new Queen lead his country to a war that will destroy it, or indulge his enemy's sole weakness: himself. **A Taboo M/M Royal Romance.**

Werewolves of Windermere:

1) **The Mating Habits of Werewolves** – Devlin is an omega with ambitions that have nothing to do with alphas, but when destiny comes calling, he may not have that much of a choice. **A/B/O, M/M/M, mpreg.**

2) **Alphas Alone** – An alpha werewolf has some responsibilities he can't ignore: finding an omega, protecting his pack, not falling for another alpha.

3) **The Parenting Habits of Werewolves** – With children in common, Devlin, Naveen and Rami know their fates are bound together, but can they find a balance beyond domesticity? And can they build a love that can last? **The conclusion to the M/M/M Mpreg Romance.**

Deep in the Dark – (Erotica by N.Y. Lysk):

- **The Weight of Duty** – Now that the twins are of age, their uncle takes them in hand to teach them their marital duties. But the experience will be very different for each of them. **Dub-con, feminization, medical body modification, abuse, group sex, arranged marriage, betrayal, incest.**

- **Soldier On** – When a humble young man is captured by the enemy lord during battle, he is expected to offer defeat to his captor by allowing him to bed him. But he is young enough that the act might unintentionally activate a hormonal process that will irreversibly feminise him. **Dub-con, Non-con, mpreg, feminization, debasement.**

- **The Will of Heaven** – Prince Hiram of Pradeira is deemed unfit to be king after his father dies. But as a direct descendant of the gods, only those of his bloodline can reign and so to avoid civil war, he agrees to have a child with each of the princes of the other noble houses of the kingdom so that his first born and heir can inherit the throne from whoever fathered him. **Dub-con, mpreg, feminization, medical kink,** debasement. *Also in German & Italian.*

- **His Brother's Dowry** – Tony agrees to accompany his brother to a new pack, knowing he will have to submit to alphas in the absence of omegas but willing to sacrifice his comfort to give Peter a chance to find love. But his brother is already in love with an omega girl and he will give anything to get her. Even Tony. **Dub-con, non-con, mpreg, feminization, debasement, body modification.**

- **The Alpha Solution** – Junen will be the next alpha of his pack... until one day he's taken by a stranger—an alpha his father rejected and who's determined to use Junen to get to him. By making him his omega. **Non-con, mpreg, kidnapping, feminization, fisting, debasement, body modification, group sex, abuse.**

ABOUT THE AUTHOR

N.J. Lysk (pronouns: whatever) is a queer one—in almost every sense of the word—for whom stories have always been their one true home. She studied linguistics and literature (which is to say, someone offered him a genuine excuse to read professionally) and ended up teaching, but writing is their one true love.

Addicted to angst, enamoured of mpreg and always ready to try a new kink (in a book, that's it!) she became hooked into the omegaverse through fanfic (but he doesn't have the patience to write other people's characters) and has recently expanded from werewolves to hockey players.

If your heart veers towards the dark, look for **N.Y. Lysk** instead & subscribe to the Dark & Taboo list[1] (these books all come with serious warnings!).

Join their mailing list at **www.njlysk.com/newsletter**[2] for book updates and free books, updates and more cool things.

Books can be acquired directly from the website at a reduced rate—new releases also become available there earlier.

---

1.   https://readerlinks.com/l/3218963

2.   **http://www.njlysk.com/newsletter**